I0603862

THE LADY IN THE BLUE DRESS

BY
EVELYN KLEBERT

The Lady in the Blue Dress
By Evelyn Klebert

A Cornerstone Book
Published by Cornerstone Book Publishers

Copyright © 2022 by Evelyn Klebert

All rights reserved under International and Pan-American Copyright Conventions. No part of this book may be reproduced in any manner without permission in writing from the copyright holder, except by a reviewer, who may quote brief passages in a review.

First Cornerstone Edition - 2022

Cornerstone Book Publishers
Hot Springs Village, AR
www.cornerstonepublishers.com

Dedication

For E.M. Poll,

A truly Great Lady
that I was blessed to have as a mother-in-law, a friend,
and a tremendous inspiration for many years.

Table of Contents

The Lady in the Blue Dress

The Bequest

The mountains in the darkness become something quite different than during the daylight hours — one seeming magnificent, awe-inspiring in their grandeur, while the other shrouded and mystical, enveloping everything within their shadow. But tonight, they appeared nothing short of ominous beneath the moonlight, exuding a nearly menacing aura — suggesting to her an ancient force that endures and aggressively remolds what it touches.

She took a quick breath, trying to jar herself out of these troubling impressions. Picking up her cell phone, she noted the time, just after eight p.m. Her heart began to beat just a slight cadence faster. It was foolish of her to be out at this time of night, foolish woman out on a foolish errand. Behind her, in the back seat, the painting lay still tightly wrapped in its packing material.

Outside the car, there was blackness everywhere — everywhere she looked. Clearly, there were no streetlights in rural Virginia, but she hadn't expected this measure of darkness. There was the one exception in the distance, which she could still see. Although it was a cloudy evening, the outline of the mountain range, the Appalachians, was still visible, not quite black, but rather a darker blue, overshadowing the countryside. Tonight, they made her feel so uneasy. When she'd arrived, she had admired their beauty, but now, they felt different, disturbing.

She followed the winding road, Bleak House Road — the name somewhat ironically suiting this strange, unreal setting she'd found herself thrust into.

Squinting through the darkness, she attempted to read the signs in front of the infrequently passed houses. Out here, it seemed everyone had so much land that each house was more like an estate, regardless of the size of the main structure. Carefully peering as she rounded a bend approaching yet another Virginia homestead, she could barely make sense of the sign hanging between two poles near the road. Engraved in the wood, it read *Blinded Moon* in an italicized script. Her heart clutched curiously at the recognition as she slowed the car at the entrance.

"The house is on the water, just past a grove of trees once you turn off the main road."

That much was true. She could see no hint of a structure in the darkness, but there was a bit of a glow further down the drive. It was astonishing that someone might actually have a light down here. She lived in a big city, and people there had lights, streetlights, lights everywhere, not this utter, morose darkness.

She calmly maneuvered her rental car down the narrow, shelled driveway. Luckily, she was creeping along because there was a sudden dip and then a quick turn around a cluster of trees. Instead of calming at the sight of the house, her heart only picked up its beat in nervousness. She was in a strange area of the country, miles away from any safety net, getting ready to meet a man she'd never laid eyes on and did not know existed until just over two months ago. And, oh yes, she was on the errand of a dead woman.

Dominique Devalieur felt rather old to be starting life over again. She'd made thirty-nine on her last birthday and had just sold her home, and, on top of that, she'd also just finished divorcing her husband of eight years. She'd also quit her teaching position at

Tulane University, set to live on her saved income while she completed research on a book on the Pre-Raphaelites in the Victorian Era. It was a contracted project, so there was a slight measure of security. And in addition to all of this, she had just buried her beloved grandmother.

She was a little at loose ends on this hot August afternoon. At present, she was staying in her grandmother's house on Freret Street in the garden district of New Orleans. She knew her occupancy would be limited while the estate was being settled. Eventually, the place would be sold, and assets that were not designated particularly amongst the heirs also sold or given away. While moderately well-off, her grandmother also had been quite the philanthropist. But for now, and purely as a stopgap, the house on Freret Street was a haven. And as everything in her life had proven to be, it was extraordinarily temporary.

The fans running along the ceiling at the Café Du Monde were doing little to stem the oppressive heat that had settled upon the city. But this was not unusual, summers in New Orleans had never been much of a picnic. She checked her watch again, deciding quite pointedly that her mother had ten more minutes to arrive then she had run out of time. Patience was something she'd become in short supply of, but then again, her mother had never done much to merit any.

From across the street, she noted a familiar figure in a white dress and a big floppy straw sunhat making her way with a group of pedestrians across the road. She sighed deeply. Part of her was honestly hoping that she wouldn't turn up. She took a sip of the café au lait — brilliant, hot coffee on a hot summer day.

The still-lithe figure in the white dress finally had maneuvered her way around the crowded patio and, without a word, started dusting what Mika assumed was white powdered sugar off the chair across from her. Her mother was approaching sixty — in fact, she had been approaching it for several years. But then, she had been married relatively young, at least on the first go-round.

Finally satisfied, she sat across from Mika and took off the hat, dropping it on the table. She was a redhead. At least, she'd been one some twenty years before. Now she was a manufactured redhead, not a drizzle or hint of gray to be found. On the other hand, Mika had several strands of gray hair, perhaps not so noticeable to the public at large, but something within her balked at the idea of covering them up. She felt, in some way, they were badges of honor threading through her wavy dark brown locks. No, she wasn't a redhead, unlike her mother or grandmother. She was the odd bird.

Patrice Dupont frowned at her, and her daughter knew instantly that she should have left. She didn't need the firing range of disapproval pointed in her direction just now. "What are you doing with yourself?" It was the first comment out of her well-lipsticked mouth.

Mika shifted in her seat, letting her eyes wander to passing tourists. How wonderful to have another life, to have another mother who comforted and supported rather than ripped to pieces like a vulture picking over a carcass. She refocused on the face before her, looking amazingly young and chipper. Maybe she'd had another Botox treatment. "Good to see you too, Mom."

She frowned. How she hated to be disregarded. "You look like hell."

She squirmed uncomfortably in the hard, well-used wooden chair. It was true. These days her appearance was one of the last considerations as she walked out the door. Of course, she had managed to dress appropriately for her grandmother's funeral yesterday. She'd worn a short-sleeved black knit dress, one of her staple outfits in teaching at Tulane. But she hadn't done that since last spring. Today, it was back to blue jeans, a button-down cotton blouse, and nope, no make-up. "Darling, you're an attractive woman. Don't act like you don't care."

She stated flatly, "I don't care," and took another sip of her coffee. The funeral yesterday had hit her much harder than she'd thought possible. It wasn't as though her grandmother's death had come as any surprise. Ostensibly for the family, she'd died some time ago. She'd been in a coma for nearly a month and in a non-communicative invalid state before that. Of course, that hadn't stopped Mika from spending hours at a time with her, holding her hand, reading to her. The doctors doubted that she realized her granddaughter was there at all. But it didn't stop her, even after she was moved to the constant care facility and then to hospice. Her grandmother had stood by her during some of the worst times of her life, been her confidant as her marriage disintegrated, and finally gave her the courage she needed to let go. So, no one and nothing could make her abandon her in her time of need, whether she was conscious of her presence or not. "I thought you said you had something important to discuss with me." She'd found it best to get down to business with her mother lest things take off on some convoluted tangent.

Again, the preoccupied frown, it was clear to Mika that as Patrice looked at her only child, what met her vision did not meet with her approval. But the truth that Patrice Dupont failed to connect with was that her daughter truly, wholly, and with no apologies, didn't care any longer. There were a minuscule group of things and people that meant something to her now, the amount of which she probably could count on one hand. Her mother simply no longer fell into that category. Too much had happened. Too much fire, and all the emotion, good and bad, was all burned out of her. "I do. I was at the reading of Mama's will this morning."

She murmured, "I thought that was a formality."

Patrice's face took on a very solemn expression that Mika found a little tough to stomach just at the moment. It was no secret to her that Patrice and her Mama had been at odds for nearly a decade, so she found more than a bit nauseating the sham of sentiment that her mother was now exhibiting. "Yes, well, for the most part, it was. Of course, you know, as soon as possible, the house will be put on the market."

Mika nodded, not surprised. Translation, pack your junk and get out ASAP. "Anything else?"

An odd expression flickered across her mother's face, something akin to irritation, but it was quickly masked. She reached into her oversized straw handbag and pulled out an envelope. For an instant, she just held it in her fingers as though she were contemplating whether or not to hand it over, and then, she impulsively flipped it down on the table.

Mika stared at the thin, business-size envelope, now sitting in a pile of powdered sugar. She didn't touch it, just asked without much emotion, "What's this?"

Patrice's voice seemed detached, "It's from Mama, for you. She left it with her will."

Mika looked at her with a slight bit of confusion. "Gran left me a bequest already. She discussed it with me long before she got sick."

Patrice let out an exasperated sigh, "Yes, well, she left you something else as well, something unexpected."

Her eyes widened a bit. "What else?"

There was a long, seemingly deliberate pause, and then she spoke sharply, "She left you the Raybourne."

With that utterance, she finally understood the inexplicable shading of Patrice Dupont's voice, the duplicitous expressions. It was quite clear what her mother felt toward her at this moment — clear, pure, unadulterated jealousy.

The Enchantress

It was curious. Even when she was quite the little girl, she had thought how very green her grandmother's eyes were. They were a strange, unusual shade, sort of dark green but with a clarity and clearness that, in later years, she'd rarely run across in any other person of her acquaintance.

Back then, when she was around eight years old, her grandfather was still alive, but her memories of him were unclear. The truth was he rarely spent time in the company of his first grandchild. But whatever his neglect might have been, his wife made up for it tenfold.

In those early years, when her parents first separated, she spent more time on Freret Street than at her own house. It had always felt more like home to her than the number of domiciles she and her mother frequented over the years.

But there was one particular day, one very memorable day, that she most treasured. It was wintertime, close to Christmas, because the fireplace downstairs was lit, and a huge white Christmas tree was sitting in that very large room. It was late at night, and she and her grandmother sat in front of the tree, sipping nearly bitter cups of hot chocolate. They had that in common. They liked their sweets laced with a tinge of bitterness.

Mika didn't know where her mother was, only that she was absent, and that seemed par for the course, even at her young age.

"Are you tired?" The lady with the dark green eyes asked her quietly. Her grandmother was dressed in a long black, plush robe with white lace. They had turned out all the lamps in the room, so they sat with the fireplace and the Christmas tree lights being the only illumination. At that moment, Mika remembered thinking her grandmother might have stepped out of some fairytale they were so fond of reading together — not as a princess but as some sort of enchantress. She always thought of her grandmother as beautiful, even as she aged.

She shook her head and sipped her chocolate, dodging a few disintegrating marshmallows in the process. "No," was all she said.

And then her enchantress smiled in a conspiratorial way and whispered back. "Would you like to see a secret?"

The question didn't surprise her much. Her grandmother was fond of secrets and did like to play. Again, she nodded back to her, saying nothing further. Back then, she was a child of few words. But then again, her grandmother seemed quite in tune with the content of whatever words she did deem to mutter. Perhaps, it was a streak of obstinacy on Mika's part, a small protest of hers against the unfair turns her life had already taken, but between them, there was an understanding. And maybe that was indeed all she needed, one who understood. Again, a whisper, "Finish your chocolate, and then I'll take you upstairs." Her grandmother leaned back in the tapestry-covered, winged-back chair she was sitting in, looking quite pleased. "Dominque, there's someone I'd like to introduce you to."

Her grandmother occupied a suite of rooms on the second floor. Her grandfather had rooms elsewhere. Mika never thought to ask about the arrangements. At that point in her young life, the idea of normalcy concerning anything was more than a bit skewed. As she got older, there wasn't much improvement.

She followed her grandmother up the rather grand, dark wooden staircase. Her pink, furry slippers slid along the highly waxed texture of the enormous surfaces. She'd measured them once. The length of two of her feet could fit on a single stair. But granted, at that age, her feet were somewhat small. She tugged on her grandmother's sleeve, suddenly feeling a little unnerved rather than excited by the mysteriousness of it all. "Who are we going to meet? Are they upstairs?"

She glanced back at her, smiling, "Patience, you must remember to savor life's surprises, my dear. Before you know it, they'll all be used up. You only get so many in a lifetime."

She remembered being struck by the elderly woman's sadness just then. And it was unusual. Her grandmother wasn't one to feel sorry for herself. She was always busy with one thing or another. And if there wasn't something to do, she created it, like their adventure tonight. Mika had a sneaking suspicion all of this was a spur-of-the-moment creation by her enchantress to amuse her, but she didn't care. She was game. And they were comrades in the storm while the madness of the outside world flew by them.

They paused on the landing, just in front of her grandmother's rooms. Mika waited and then finally inquired, "Is it in your bedroom?"

She shook her head, "No, it's in another place. A small room I've never taken you to before. I wanted to wait until you were old enough. "

Silently, they traveled down the hallway past the large doors to the suite and stopped in front of a smaller door at the end of the hall. Mika was sure she'd passed it before, but it was so nondescript, just an ordinary, white wooden door. No doubt, she had assumed it was a closet. There seemed to be nothing special about it. The house was full of them.

Again, they paused, probably a bit longer than was merited. So, she asked, having the forthrightness of a child that had yet to learn the world's subtlety. "What sort of room is it?"

Her grandmother's fingertips lightly brushed the doorknob, but then she dropped her hand, seemingly indecisive. "It's my special place. I keep it just for myself, but I think you would appreciate it."

Mika looked up at her quite solemnly as she remembered and answered, "I'm sure I will."

Quietly, her grandmother reached up and opened the door. The entrance was relatively narrow, but she gently pushed Mika forward. At first, it was impossible to see, and her foot slammed into something. Behind her, her grandmother put a hand on her shoulder. "There's two steps inward. Be careful." They were steep steps. Mika took them awkwardly and then gratefully found herself on flatter ground. She heard the door being swung shut behind them. And then another whisper, "Are you ready for one of your life's surprises?"

She nodded, just now very anxious to get out of the darkness. She heard a lamp on the wall switch on as the room suddenly was illuminated by a soft light. It took a moment, or maybe a few, to focus on everything she saw. There was an old-fashioned, apothecary-looking desk against the wall, and across from it, bookshelves with volumes and ornaments, as well as lovely small porcelain statues. Then across the little room was a great bay window that was just streaming in the slightest bit of moonlight. Beneath it was a velvet window seat with plush, lovely, soft pillows. In the first moments, as she took it in, all of it felt so comforting, cared for, and special. "This is a beautiful room," she whispered, genuinely enchanted. "You must love having this room."

And then, quite calmly, her grandmother said, "This is not my room. I made it for her."

She smoothly gestured with her hand in a way that reminded Mika again of the enchantress casting a spell. She pointed behind

Mika's back, making her realize that there was one wall of the room that she'd failed to examine. She turned around slowly and then just stopped. "You see, my dearest. This room is for the Lady in the Blue Dress."

Mika didn't remember if she gasped. Her heart must have skipped a few beats because she saw something within that ornate golden frame that her grandmother saw as well — something so special and unique only to them. Later, it would become clear to her that not everyone shared their passion for this painting. Some only saw it as a commodity, her mother a prime example. But she and her grandmother saw something well beyond that. They saw magic.

The Raybourne

The actual name of the painting was not the Lady in the Blue Dress, as her grandmother was fond of calling it, but rather *The Burning Candle*. It was the work of an English painter by the name of Henry Joseph Raybourne at the turn of the century in 1902. He, Mika was to find in later years, followed in the footsteps of a somewhat reformist group of painters during the Victorian era in England. They rebelled against the constrictive mandates of the Royal Society of Art, determined to paint with objectives born before the ideals commonly embraced by the work of the artist Raphael. The group sought to return to the intense detail, vibrant color, and complicated compositions of Quattrocento Italian art.

Mika crafted many substantial articles on the subject, submitting to a collection of historical journals. Even now, she was knee-deep into her book on the personal history of the Pre-Raphaelites. Something during that night so long ago had fueled her imagination, and curiously, she'd felt as though somehow her grandmother's Lady in the Blue Dress had walked beside her all her life.

The painting itself was quite amazing — the lovely introspective, mysterious dark-haired female in a long dark blue velvet dress, with an embroidered tapestry-like bodice at the waist, holding a crystal ball. Only feet away from her on a desk sat what seemed to be a wand, a large goblet, a burning candle, and, perhaps most shocking, a human skull. The skull itself became pivotal to the history of the painting. At some point, it was acquired by a private collector who had a curtain painted over the skull and some of the other objects on the desk. A later owner discovered the deception and restored it to its original state. Sometime after, no one was sure how, her grandmother acquired the treasured painting. It became clear, very early on to Mika how precious it was to her. Her grandmother was unyieldingly protective of it, not for its value but perhaps because she felt, on some level, it was vulnerable. Mika wasn't sure exactly why, except that her grandmother had viewed the altering of the painting as an aberrant attack against the Lady in the Blue Dress. That the woman could be an eccentric was a given, but there was never anything dulled about her grandmother's wits. She was always sharp as a fine pinprick, so razored that you never felt it pierce the skin but could definitely see blood in its aftermath.

There was a concrete walking park along the riverfront. It was a hot day, and Mika slowly meandered through the area, gazing out at the active waters of the Mississippi River. There was a bit of a fluttering within her. All of this was a surprise. Her grandmother had always been successful in pulling these off. She clutched the envelope in question in her hand, and the painting that hung in that special room on Freret Street now would find a home with her. She would become the guardian of the Lady in the Blue Dress. She'd never dared to hope that it would be so. It was unfathomable how much money that painting represented. But to her, it meant much more. It represented a sign of hope for a life that had gone deeply off the tracks.

She settled on one of the cement benches in the park, not yet willing to open the envelope. She had no idea what it might be. Her mother seemed so put out that she didn't open it in her presence. It was clear that the fact that the painting had been bequeathed to her daughter instead of herself profoundly chaffed her. "You know it isn't right that Mama left it to only you. It is her most potentially valuable asset. At the least, it should be sold and divided among all her heirs."

But Mika had sat there, hardly listening, so shocked was she by this turn of events. They'd never discussed it. Her grandmother had never even hinted that she would leave it to her. In some ways, the painting had inspired a lifetime of work for Mika, but she'd viewed it as a blessing, not an entitlement.

So rather quickly, she had excused herself, collecting her envelope and leaving a somewhat stunned mother behind.

As she sat gazing out at the water, she breathed deeply, lightly touching the envelope that she knew had been in her grandmother's hands at one point. She didn't want to hurry to it but instead savor all the emotions. This might well be the final meeting for the comrades. And she didn't want to say goodbye, to wander the tumultuous earth without her guide.

Finally, she slipped her finger beneath the place where it was sealed so that she could release its contents. It made her smile. Her grandmother was well off. She could certainly afford an embossed envelope, even with a seal, but instead, she chose a generic, unmemorable carrier for her final message to her granddaughter. If she was anything, she was not pretentious.

There were two pages of lined paper within. She recognized her grandmother's script. Quite regularly, while she was away at college, she would receive cards and letters in the mail from her. Mika remembered looking forward to them, as they had the power to bolster her spirits and confidence as nothing else seemed capable of doing.

Quite gingerly, she opened the pages. She knew they were destined to become priceless pieces of memorabilia that she would save all her days.

The letter began,

Dearest One,

For you to be getting this, I am sure I have embarked on another journey. My only regret is that you won't be sharing this particular adventure with me. But that is the only one. I have no fear of what is coming, only anticipation. I have been done with this world for years, it seems, just biding my time until another door opened for me.

But you, my child, are not done with this world yet. I know there has been much disappointment for you. But there is happiness to be found. And I, in quiet moments when all the clamor around me dissipates, know that you will find it. Please trust in that.

Now there is another matter. I have one more thing that I need from you. And knowing you, it could very well be the most challenging request I have ever asked of you. But all my faith is in your honesty and goodness. And I am sure you will honor my wishes.

As I know you have been told, I have left the lady in your safe hands. What you don't know is that it is not my intention that it stay there.

Mika felt a sudden stab of shock. So startled was she that she quickly reread the line to confirm what it said.

I am sure it would have no safer haven than with you, my angel, but I have left it to you, knowing that you were the only one I could trust with my wishes.

For reasons I can't begin to explain to you now, there is another place, another person, who deserves her more than you and I.

There is a man whose whereabouts I will include in this letter. He is where the painting belongs. I realize what I ask is very hard for you. But I trust you and know clearly as though I am there to see that you will follow my request. There are reasons I chose to handle things this way. Perhaps in time, you will understand. Just know you have always been closest to my heart.

Love,

Your Gran, Adele St. Clair

At the bottom of the page was written a name and address. She just sat there for some time, feeling the tightness in her throat and stemming the tears that wanted to fall. It seemed her grandmother wasn't done with surprising her, not quite yet.

James Clairmont

She killed the headlights of her rental car and then turned off the engine. A light was on near the house's front door, but no one emerged. Even now, she questioned her decision to come here at all, questioned her decision to deliver the Lady in the Blue Dress into the hands of a stranger. In some ways, it felt akin to parceling off a member of her family to an unknown party. The truth was, sadly, it might be much easier to part with some of her family.

She let her head rest on the steering wheel. Even though the air conditioner wasn't on, a chill had passed through the car. It was already getting cold, but it was only early autumn. It had taken nearly two and a half months of soul-wrenching discussions with her conscience to get her here at all.

When Mika first saw his name on the bottom of her grandmother's letter, it didn't really register with her. The whole matter she tried to put out of her mind as she focused on moving out of the house on Freret Street. Within a week after her grandmother's funeral, she had leased a spacious townhouse on St. Charles Avenue. Before leaving her the Lady in the Blue Dress, her grandmother's bequest and her divorce settlement had left her well able to take unemployed respites and lease more than comfortable lodgings.

Without much fanfare, she obtained the proper packing materials and quietly moved the Raybourne painting to her new home. She put it in her bedroom. She'd promised herself she would enjoy a month with it before following Adele St. Clair's last wishes. Quickly enough, one month slipped into two, and then it became quite comfortable to drop the whole scheme and leave things as they were. That was, of course, until the dreams began.

It was peculiar, unfamiliar, where she was walking because the earth here was red, a wet red clay beneath her bare feet. The air was cold, chilled all around her. As she walked, the small sticks and dried leaves she stepped on pinched into her flesh painfully, but she continued upward. She was forced to push against the slim tree trunks to propel herself forward, up the hill as it became steeper. And, of course, there was that damp red earth everywhere, slippery — not like back home. It didn't occur to her at the time that this was not real. Dreams are not like that. They live and breathe in the moment and, in that moment, feel as solid and tangible as anything in the waking world.

When she finally came to the crest of the hill, she stopped and looked out over the tranquil water. There was a peacefulness, and she deeply breathed in the cool air. The voice whispered in her ears, *Seek.* She looked around at the forest. Then in the fraction of an instant, in the measure of thought, it sprang alive in movement. The branches, the leaves, suddenly animated, and worse than that, the shadows — long tendrils springing to life, wrapping around her like tight, thin snakes squeezing the very breath out of her.

Then there was a loud crash. She sat up in the bed, completely disoriented. In the semi-darkness of the room, as her eyes quickly focused, she could see clearly that the painting had fallen from the wall onto the desk that was situated beneath it. Her heart began hammering in sheer panic. What would she do if she'd damaged it? It didn't make sense. It was perfectly secure when she'd hung it on the wall.

With shaking hands, she lifted it upwards. There was a slight discoloration of the frame, but miraculously the picture was undamaged. A coldness of realization crept into her stomach. It whispered to her that it was all right this time, but the picture wasn't hers to keep. So, it wouldn't be safe with her.

The following day after scarcely any sleep, two cups of coffee, and her grandmother's letter in hand, she called information for James Clairmont of Earlysville, Virginia. As she listened to her cell phone ringing, she nervously clicked her fingernails on the cherry wood desk that the painting had fallen onto the night before. She stared up at the Lady in the Blue Dress, saying a silent prayer that she was doing the right thing.

"Hello." She swallowed, something catching in her throat at the sound of the masculine voice on the other end of the line. Again, "Hello, is anyone there?"

"Yes, I'm sorry. I'd like to speak to James Clairmont."

There was a bit of silence, then finally, "May I ask who is calling?"

"Um, yes, my name is Dominique Devalieur. But he might be more familiar with my grandmother's name, Adele St. Clair."

There was another prolonged silence, and she wondered if he was still there. "This is James Clairmont."

"Oh, I see. "

"The name St. Clair is familiar to me. I believe my uncle mentioned an acquaintance of that name."

She paused again, wondering the reason for all of this. "I see. I don't really know how to say this Mr. Clairmont, so I'll just plunge in. My grandmother died a few months ago."

"I'm very sorry for your loss, but I'm not following —"

"Well, my grandmother left a significant and personal possession to me, and then in a letter after she passed away, she asked me to give that possession to you. And I was wondering if you could tell me why."

There was another agonized silence. Mika was waiting for him to launch into the — *"Are you quite out of your mind? What is your problem?"* and finally, what she really hoped, *"Please don't bother me with this."* But the next thing she heard wasn't nearly what she expected. "I understand."

She waited for elaboration, but there was none offered. "What does that mean? Do you know something of this matter, Mr. Clairmont?"

Again, she waited through a protracted pause and then, "Ms. Devalieur, this possession wouldn't happen to be a painting, would it?"

She just sat there. She was quite sure if she looked at herself, she would see her jaw hanging open. Then after an impossibly long stunned silence, she finally asked, "How do you know that?"

"Quite honestly, I was told the Raybourne painting would be coming back into the family soon."

"I-I don't understand, Mr. Clairmont. Were you in contact with my grandmother, or was someone else in your family?" There was an odd feeling of panic that had surfaced around her heart area.

Another silence, and completely sidestepping her question, he asked, "When did you say your grandmother died, Ms. Devalieur?"

"Early July." Now she felt uncomfortable. "I'm sorry I didn't move on this more quickly, but my personal life has been somewhat chaotic."

"No explanations necessary. How would you like to handle things?" The strange fluctuations of this conversation she found very unnerving.

"Mr. Clairmont," she sighed rather audibly, "To tell you the truth, I hadn't thought things out. This painting was very important to my grandmother. The only reason I'm doing this at all is that she asked me to. And to be frank, I have no idea why."

"But you're willing to do it anyway." He commented directly to the point.

"Yes, it is her last wish, and I can't ignore it. No matter how odd it seems to me."

"It's clear she chose the right person for this particular task."

She wiped away a wayward tear that had fallen down her cheek. She suddenly had become choked up by the turn of the conversation that chaffed at a wound that had not yet had time to heal. "I don't know. I suppose I could have it shipped to you."

He was quiet again and replied, "I suppose it could be done that way, but I think it would be better if you brought it yourself."

She waited, trying to discern if she'd heard him correctly. "You mean come to Virginia?"

"Yes, that's what I mean."

That possibility hadn't even occurred to her. "I-I don't know. I do have obligations here." Actually, her mind was flying across the fact that there were so few obligations at present.

"Perhaps, you could schedule some time away. It's beautiful country here, particularly this time of year."

"I don't know." It seemed too much of a leap. After all, he was a stranger.

"Well, why don't you think about it? I'll call you back later in the week. I have your number on my phone."

"Okay, I guess that would be all right."

"Good, and Ms. Devalieur."

"Yes."

"Don't worry. It will work out fine."

That night Mika dreamt about the hillside again, but this time it was even colder, winter perhaps. She sat quietly against a tree, watching the snow slowly fall and cover the frozen lake. She was sure she was talking to someone, but she had no idea exactly who.

What's wrong?

I'm tired.

Tired of what?

Living, I suppose. Nothing I do seems to work.

Maybe you're doing the wrong things.

That's helpful. What are the right things?

The breeze around her moved and circled her in a comforting way in response to her despairing thoughts. *Move forward. That is the only way to live.*

Two nights later, she was typing up some research notes for her book when the phone rang.

"Hello."

"Ms. Devalieur, it's James Clairmont. I hope I'm not interrupting you."

"No, it's fine. I could use an interruption."

"Working hard?"

"Uhm, sort of. I'm doing research for a book I'm writing."

"I see, a writer. That must be interesting." He sounded relaxed to her as though he were settling into an easy conversation with an old acquaintance.

"Well, not as interesting as one might think. Do you work?" Quickly, she realized what an awkward question that was.

"Well, as little as possible." She heard distinct amusement in his voice. She couldn't pinpoint it, but there seemed to be a hint of an accent there, not southern, a bit clipped, as though he came from somewhere north.

"I'm sorry. I suppose that didn't sound too good."

"Actually, I'm a translator. I translate books, documents, whatever is needed from other languages into English."

"That sounds interesting. What languages?"

"Well, many. I work in at least half a dozen."

"Really? Now that's impressive." He must be well-educated for that sort of work. She found that comforting. At least, he might recognize the value of what he'd be receiving.

"Not really, but it does pay the bills. Have you considered my proposal?"

She shifted a bit in the chair, surprised at how quickly he got to the point. "No, I've been busy. I haven't really thought about it."

"Haven't thought about it or haven't made a decision?"

She smiled, too perceptive. "Honestly, haven't made a decision."

"Understandable. May I ask you a question?"

"I suppose."

"Your grandmother Adele, did she call you Dominique?"

She swallowed a bit nervously, "No, she didn't. She called me Mika."

"Well, I'm a bit uncomfortable with formality. Since we've become tied in a fashion by these unusual circumstances, how about you call me James, and I'll call you Mika?"

She wasn't sure how the request for familiarity hit her, but she decided to try to take advantage of it anyway. "All right, but now I'd like you to tell me how you knew about the painting."

"Ah, good question, and I promise to answer that when I see you."

"Now, that's not fair."

"No, it's not, but it gives me a little leverage. But think about it, Mika. Do you think your grandmother would ask you to give such a valuable possession to someone less than trustworthy?"

She considered his statement for a moment, then fired back flatly. "I have no idea why she has asked me to do this. There are about a thousand scenarios that I could come up with."

"Well, creative too, but I do see your point. Maybe you should sleep on it a few more nights."

"Maybe." She knew she must have sounded somewhat abrupt with him. She was feeling just a bit irritated as well as somewhat cornered, not a pleasant combination.

"Well then, I'll say goodnight, Mika."

"Goodnight."

She hung up the phone, feeling a strange quivering inside, as though something in her very predictable world had fallen off-balance.

"So, you've decided."

She frowned, wondering if, indeed, that was the case. "What makes you say that?"

"Just a hunch. I don't sense that you're a woman that likes to keep loose ends dangling for too long."

She sipped the green tea she'd finished brewing only moments before the phone rang. She had no idea why, but all day long, she carried the feeling that she'd be speaking to him tonight. Strangely, it never occurred to her to call him. But as she settled down at her desk to start typing the introduction to her book, the phone did ring. "Well, I wouldn't put money on that. I wasted eight years on a bad marriage."

"That must have been difficult."

She spun a little in her office chair. Why had she mentioned that to him? "I'm sorry. I didn't mean to bring that up."

"I'm glad you did. It tells me that it might be you trust me just a little."

She smiled, "Maybe just a little."

Since she'd started, she decided to continue in that vein, "So, are you married?" Now, didn't that sound awkward?

There was a slight laugh on the other end. Well, at least she was amusing. "No, I'm not," then his voice became a tinge more somber. "I was married years ago, but my wife died."

"Oh, I'm sorry."

"It was some time ago."

"I guess I seem like I'm prying."

"I think we're just getting to know each other cautiously, but maybe moving a little closer."

"This trip, you know, it's a bit out of character for me." It was another confession. But oddly, talking to someone like this, with so much distance, felt safe.

"I gathered that." He said rather matter-of-factly. Sometimes he acted too much as if he knew what to expect from her.

"I just have to admit I'm curious about what's behind all of this."

"Maybe we can find some answers when you get here. Why don't you make your plans and then let me know the details."

"All right."

"Don't worry, Mika. It might actually work out very well."

She was a little girl wandering through the shadowed house on Freret Street. Everything was dim, only illuminated by an occasional candle on the furniture. She tried to call out for someone but, at the moment, couldn't seem to speak.

As though compelled, she ran up the steps toward the secret room on the second floor. When she touched it lightly with her hands, the door gave way easily and swung open.

This room, too, was only lit by candles that cast drapes of flickering shadows across everything.

Something was wrong. She knew it at once, the tingling of fear acutely traveling along her skin. No one was here, but she felt as though someone was.

Slowly, she turned around to look at the painting. It was there, hanging on the wall, but something was horribly wrong. Moving closer, she sought to verify what she thought she was seeing.

It was true, but it was insane.

Everything was there — the desk, the goblet, the candle, the skull, the wand — everything except the Lady in the Blue Dress. Quite shockingly, it was as though she had just dropped out of the portrait.

She stood there transfixed, unable to move, and suddenly felt a hand touch her bare arm. Slowly turning around and trembling with terror, she first saw the velvet sleeve of the blue dress and then stared into eyes that were black as midnight but filled with sparkling light. She was absolutely paralyzed but at the same time being drawn into power. And oddly, it felt familiar. But it was too much. All of it was too much, and she opened her mouth to scream.

When she awoke, she was still screaming, sitting in her bed. Across the room, the painting still hung on the wall as it had always been. She sat there shaking, covered in a cold sweat. She lay back in bed and stared at the ceiling for some time before she allowed sleep to retake her.

Virginia

She had booked a room at the Omni hotel on the downtown mall in Charlottesville, Virginia. The Omni came highly recommended on the web, and any place that said it was near any kind of mall sounded like a haven to her. Earlysville, where James Clairmont lived, was just on the outskirts of Charlottesville. Some two weeks after that most disturbing dream, she and the Lady in the Blue Dress were on a flight to Virginia.

The hotel room was nice, on the fifth floor, with a decent view of the outdoor mall and its brick-laid street below. No, of course, it couldn't rival the opulent hotels on Canal Street and around the French Quarter, but it was a welcome change of pace. On the queen-sized bed lay the Raybourne painting, still well-packaged from the flight. Things had gone smoothly, but she still hadn't called him. The last time she spoke to James Clairmont, she'd been vague about her plans. In her convoluted reasoning, she wanted to leave herself a backdoor. If her uncemented arrival was inconvenient for some reason, then the deal was off. And she would consider herself entirely free of the obligation.

On the other hand, even she had to admit that the painting had taken on a bit of an ominous aura since her odd dream. It all was perplexing. But the memory remained as vivid and fresh as though she had just awoken screaming.

She checked her watch. It was nearly seven at night. With some hesitation, she picked up her cell phone from the end table beside the bed and clicked on his number.

She waited, calmly tapping her foot. She was completely and utterly divided. She had no idea if she wanted him to pick up or not. It was hard to admit to herself, but she had not gained a sure footing since, well, since her marriage disintegrated and then her grandmother got sick. All had begun to spin out of control around her, and now that disordered, whirlwind state had oddly become the norm.

"Hello."

She swallowed painfully. "James."

"Yes, Mika."

"I-I know I didn't give you any notice, but I'm in town."

There was a pause. No doubt she'd caught him off guard. She waited nervously, having no idea what to expect. "So, you're here. Well, you are a woman of surprises." He did sound pleased. So strange that it was like a balm to an open wound to hear someone so happy to hear from her.

"I guess I'm a bit impulsive."

"I admire that trait. Where are you staying?"

"The Omni."

"Nice, that's right in the heart of everything."

"Well," she murmured, "I'm a city girl. It's comforting."

"So, tell me, when can I see you?"

Her eyes glanced across the well-wrapped painting that lay across the bed. "I have the Raybourne. When would you like it?"

"Hmm, I'd very much like to see you and the Raybourne tonight. Would you like me to pick you up?"

Her heart picked up its beat. She hadn't expected it to be so soon. Tonight? "Um, no, I have a car. You can give me directions."

"Are you sure? I'm a bit out of the way."

"That's fine. Just give me instructions, and I have a GPS. I want to learn my way around the area."

"Alright, if you're sure, this place might be different from what you're used to."

"Don't worry. I can handle myself."

"Well, I'm glad to hear it."

She shouldn't have dragged her feet about leaving, but she did, reluctant again to turn over the painting. In the end, though, she began her trek with a GPS that had decided to stop working and more than a few confusing turns. But despite that, it had ended here, parked in the driveway, in front of his house with the darkness covering everything like a blanket, except the soft lights coming from the porch. The night around her was palpable. She closed her eyes, saying a prayer, a rarity admittedly for her, but she asked if she was doing the wrong thing, for someone or something to please stop her before it was too late.

And then she glanced up, and there was movement. The front door swung open, and a tall figure stepped out into the semi-darkness of the shelled driveway. As she watched him, it was indeed as though, for a moment, she had stopped breathing.

How she'd gotten here now seemed like an inconceivable bend in her life, unforeseeable indeed. But then again, nothing, not a thing along her life's journey thus far, had turned out as she'd imagined it would.

The figure just stood there, waiting. Feeling as though it was her move, Mika opened the car door and stepped out into the driveway.

He spoke to her, still some yards away. "Coming in, or are you still debating?"

She shrugged, "I don't feel like braving these dark roads again, not yet anyway."

And then he wandered more closely to her, although his face was still in shadows. "People around here seem to have something against too many lights."

"So, I gathered." Feeling quite awkward, she held out her hand. "I'm Mika Devalieur."

And he grasped hers in return in a warm, secure grip that surprised her, though why she couldn't quite put together. "I didn't tell you before, but that might be the loveliest name I've ever run across."

She laughed, feeling even more awkward now, "Um, thanks, James, I hope." The thought that this man wasn't James Clairmont had never seriously occurred to her. The voice certainly matched — low but smooth, polished would be an apt description.

"Yes, why don't you come inside."

And then she hesitated, "The painting, it's in the car."

She moved quickly to the passenger door to open it. She felt him watching her closely, but she continued. It was far better to get it over with before there were more second thoughts. She gently lifted the painting off the seat and, stepping away from the car, closed the door behind her. He made no motion to take the painting from her. Oddly, she felt he sensed how difficult this would be for her. "Come inside, Mika," was all he said.

And then he moved toward the house, leaving her to follow.

His home itself was purely what could be called the antithesis of the house on Freret Street. While her grandmother's home was in every way linked to the past and shadows, this place was filled with light and sharp tones of the present. Once entering through a short hallway, they passed an airy open kitchen that flowed directly into an informal dining room with a large table whose wood was just shy of white. There were other rooms on the way, but they were moving quickly toward the center of the house, a huge den whose ceiling went up for two floors closing in on a tremendous skylight. She paused and took a breath, a bit overwhelmed by what she saw. She had no idea what she'd expected, but it wasn't this. She was completely caught off-guard.

Standing beside her, he asked, "Do you want to put that down? It must be getting heavy." She'd forgotten for a moment that she was still holding the precious parcel. His voice drew her focus more acutely on the man beside her, of who she now had an unobstructed view.

He was tall as she'd noted outside, at least six feet, casually dressed — blue jeans and a long-sleeved, cream-colored shirt made of some very soft material that she couldn't place at the moment. His hair was dark, not quite black, and he wore a short-cropped beard and mustache. From first inspection, she estimated he was around her age, if not a bit older. He remained there calmly as though waiting for her to make a move. She smiled, and a strong wave of fatigue hit her. Maybe it signaled the relaxing of some very taught nerves, but she wasn't sure. "Where do you want it?" She asked directly.

He moved toward her now, gently taking the painting out of her hands and brushing her fingers in the process. She glanced down, a bit embarrassed. "Well, why don't we see how she's made the voyage?"

She nodded and followed him as he took another doorway into the dining room that she'd glimpsed briefly before. While he began to unwrap the painting carefully, she glanced around. It was an odd mixture of pale woods and black, stark contrasts. There was a pen and ink landscape of the area she suspected on the wall. "Are you feeling all right, Mika?" He murmured as he continued the task at hand.

His inquiry startled her for some reason. It felt strange, as though it put them on a more personal footing that she wasn't sure their acquaintance warranted. "I'm a bit tired, I suppose. I feel like I've been on a bit of a roller coaster."

He glanced up from his work, and it struck her. His eyes were a very distinct blue, clear but rather dark. "You can relax now," he said.

"Really?" She shot him a glance that was reputed to put colleagues and ex-husbands on guard.

But James Clairmont seemed slightly amused by it, "Yes." And then he continued pulling off the final wrapping that covered the surface.

Mika watched him as he stared at the painting with little expression, but then again, he did seem to be studying it. Unexpectedly, for an instant, he passed his fingertips near the surface of the lady's face and then slowly withdrew them again.

Mika forced herself to look again at the Lady in the Blue Dress, knowing it was most probably for the last time. An obstruction of grief seemed to form in her throat spontaneously. All she could see before her was her grandmother's delight when she first showed Mika the painting in her special room so long ago.

She felt irrational anger boil up at so many things, this relinquishing of her grandmother's treasure just being the icing on the cake. Oddly, the man beside her reached over and touched her arm as though he sensed what she was thinking. "It will be all right, Mika."

She deliberately stepped away from him. "Strange that you can say that with conviction, Mr. Clairmont, especially since we are strangers." She picked up her purse from a nearby cabinet where she'd placed it when she'd first entered the room.

He eyed her directly, "You're leaving?"

"Yes, you have your painting. And there's no reason for me to stay. However, I would like you to keep your bargain and answer my question. Tell me why my grandmother did this."

He frowned a bit as though this was unexpected, "That's not a short answer. How about you put down your purse, and I make you a cup of tea?"

She glanced up at the black clock on the wall. "It's getting late."

He smiled disarmingly, "Night is my most productive time."

Bleak House Road

leak House Road wasn't the best place to live. In many respects, it was a poor choice for someone like him. That was the beauty of it. No one expected him to be here.

Of course, one had to be on guard constantly, but then again, it did force him to sharpen his awareness — sort of like living amid a battleground, albeit a deceptive battleground. Calm, beautiful, tranquil on the surface, but beneath was another story.

Perhaps, it was ill-advised to allow the granddaughter to come out here so soon. But he was curious about a great many things. So, he did what was ill-advised. He invited her.

She was standing in front of his picture window overlooking the Rivanna River, but certainly, she couldn't see it through the darkness. He wondered with distraction if she could feel it at all, what lurked around them. At times, he thought he was beginning to sound like one of the madmen out of an Edgar Allan Poe story. Anytime now, he was sure he'd start hearing the rap, tap, tapping at his chamber door.

He frowned pensively. Mika was quite unusual looking, somewhat exotic with her large brandy-colored eyes and dark wavy hair. But brittle, which he picked up too. So brittle that if you pushed her the wrong way, all the pieces might fall apart. That was no good. It wouldn't do for what was coming.

He walked up beside her and handed her a cup of tea. Her hands were small, delicate, as though they had no strength, but he felt this was surely an illusion. There was power here. That was clear. She looked up at him with suspicion lurking in those wide brown orbs. Yes, there was an awareness too. "Thank you," it came out in nearly a whisper.

He smiled, "It's hot. Don't let it scorch you."

She glanced around, "Your house is quite impressive. Have you been here long?"

He shook his head. "Two years." Two very long years, not unlike self-imposed seclusion.

"And before that?" she inquired. She was digging. Good girl, her mind was intensely quick and alert to subtlety. That too was clear.

"Boston, Baltimore, even Edinburgh for a while."

An eyebrow rose, "Scotland? Really, what brought you there?"

"I went to college for a while in my twenties."

She smiled, responding to that, "That sounds wonderful," perhaps a romantic lurked beneath all that cynicism.

"It's quite an old place, filled with history."

She looked again out into the darkness. James looked too but tried not to focus. At this time of night, there was too much to see. She sipped her tea again, and he glanced away. He thought with some confidence that it probably wouldn't take too long for the herb he'd slipped in it to take effect.

She sat on the couch in James Clairmont's den across from the fireplace. The mantle was impressive in tones of black, brown, and beige, a marbleized stone, rustic but elegant. That, she supposed, was an apt description for the house itself, rustic but elegant. Even the sofa she was sitting on seemed to fit that category, a dark blue suede, surprisingly comfortable. He was sitting near her in a chair of the same tone. At the moment, he was quiet, seeming content simply to let her absorb her surroundings. "This is a lovely house," she murmured. Hadn't she said that already? It wasn't like her to repeat herself.

"It's comfortable."

"Where are you going to put it?" she asked. Then she realized she must be sounding a bit incoherent. "The painting, I mean."

"Oh, I hadn't thought about it."

"It doesn't suit this place." Had she said that out loud? She'd thought it but certainly hadn't meant to voice it.

"Well, the truth is I don't intend to be here forever." His voice seemed oddly distant, although he wasn't far at all.

"Oh, you're going to be leaving here then?"

"Eventually," was his answer. He'd become much less communicative since they'd come to sit in the den. Strange, but then again, everything about this was strange.

She placed her cup of tea on the coffee table in front of her. It had become actually heavy in her hand, but it didn't matter. She'd finished it.

"How long were you married, Mika?"

Her eyes widened a bit. "Um, eight years." Seemed like an unexpected question, wasn't she supposed to ask him something, something about the painting? "It didn't work out. I mean, it didn't seem bad, not until the end, but it was. I don't know, lonely somehow, I suppose."

He nodded, "I see."

"You said your wife died." she straightened up but suddenly felt dizzy. Maybe she was getting sick.

"Yes, a long time ago."

"That must have been hard."

"Yes, she was a good friend," he answered.

"A friend?" So uncensored. That wasn't like her to be so unguarded with her thoughts.

"Yes, I suppose we were more friends than anything."

She considered what he'd said, sadly reflecting on her life. "My husband and I weren't really friends, not for a long time. I guess that would be a good basis for a marriage."

He watched her so intently, in a way that made her nervous, "It's one kind of marriage."

She glanced at the clock. It was close to nine, and she knew she had to drive back through all that darkness. "I think I should get going. It's late." She stood up but caught the arm of the couch as another wave of dizziness swept over her. He had also gotten to his feet and grasped her arm firmly with his hand. "Are you feeling all right?"

She looked into his dark blue eyes, "I don't know. I'm feeling strange." And then he was holding both her arms.

"It's too late for you to be out," he murmured.

His words seemed puzzling to her. "What do you mean?"

"It wouldn't be safe."

"Safe?" she repeated. "I don't understand."

The dizziness kept coming, now more potent, in waves, but she still heard his voice. "It's best you stay tonight."

"I can't."

She slumped against his chest, no longer able to stand unaided. He whispered into her ear. "Don't fight it. It will be all right." And then she felt swept up into his arms before she completely collapsed.

There was no light, just blackness. She ran frantically deep into the woods. Though she could not see it, she felt it all around her. The trees snagged at her clothes, branches catching, tearing, pulling, almost as though they were actively trying to impede her progress. Chilling fear forced her to push forward, always forward. She didn't know the way out, only that she had to keep moving. Still, the twigs, leaves, and wood grabbed at her with long, sharp, dagger-like fingers, not trying to disguise themselves. The cuts and scratches on her arms, legs, and face burned, but it only drove her into a wilder panic. Overhead, the sky was masked by a dark cloudy cover. There was no light, no light anywhere to guide her. They were growing in strength, the fingers tightening like cold dark hands, pulling her, pulling her down, smothering. She struggled, thrashing outward with wild, mindless terror.

She heard him whispering, brushing her forehead gently with his fingertips. "Calm," he murmured, "calm." Her eyes flickered open and blurrily focused on the dim light of the room. Above her, a ceramic fan on a paneled ceiling was slowly turning. The breath she tried to take felt impeded, sluggish, and painful.

She questioned his presence, not unconvinced she was still dreaming, perhaps dreaming everything. But he seemed to be there, sitting on the edge of the bed, lightly touching her hand, then her forehead again in a soothing motion. "You mustn't try to leave right now," he whispered. "They are powerful tonight and desperate."

Her throat felt sore, making it difficult to speak. "What's going on?" That was all she managed.

He spoke softly, murmuring something she didn't understand —another language, it seemed, but not focused on her. Profound sleepiness quickly began to take her over. "It's all right. Rest now."

Her eyes closed again. She couldn't seem to do anything to stop it. But her arms and body still stung from the scratches and clawing of the forest.

He felt confident that she was safe for the time being, so he left her. He felt weary all the way into his bones. It made sense upon reflection that they would attack so relentlessly. They sensed her here, sensed the vulnerability. And they hungered and feared. Of course, he'd anticipated this might happen, but he also knew it was necessary. A significant chain of events that began long ago was about to be set into motion. And just like a well-played chess match, all the pieces needed to be in place.

He returned to where the painting lay on the dining room table. Mika was right, of course. It didn't belong here, but then, did any of them? He brought a large candle from the sideboard, lit it, and then turned off the lights. He sat in front of the painting, staring at it intensely, now allowing his abilities to look deeply. Immediately, he saw movement and emanations from the figure. Being here, near them both, was stirring the spirit. He shook his head, honestly not knowing if he was pleased or not. But it lived. Despite everything, it still lived.

A Lucky Woman

Adele St. Clair was a lucky young woman. She had married well, into a prominent family, and her husband was a major in the army at only twenty-seven. That in itself was an accomplishment. She lived in quite a large, excellently furnished house on Freret Street that George had inherited from his grandfather. Earlier in the year, she had just turned twenty-three. By any standards, everyone would say that she was indeed a lucky woman.

Today, she'd taken the streetcar to Canal Street to do some shopping. It was a lovely October morning. George had just left for Europe yesterday. His leave for several weeks had ended rather quickly, it seemed. Her mother had cautioned her about going out alone. After all, the country was in the middle of a war, and the city was filled with soldiers. But Adele seldom listened to her mother these days. Of course, she had taken her advice concerning her marriage and had taken advantage of the opportunity to marry upward. But now, at present, she wasn't as open to advice. With her husband away, she felt emancipated in some tangible way. There was freedom in that. She had seen George off at the train station that morning, watching tearful heart-wrenching goodbyes taking place all about her, and yet, she'd felt oddly untouched by it all. After all, her husband was a bit of a stoic man, and she had always found her emotions not easily stirred.

She wandered, strolling by the large buildings on Canal Street — Maison Blanche, Godchaux's, and Kreeger's — finally stopping in

D.H. Holmes, remembering a china pattern her mother-in-law wanted her to consider replacing hers with. She drifted about, looking everywhere but not really seeing. Something subtle was brewing within her, quite assuredly, but she couldn't put her finger on precisely what it could be.

It was curious to feel so discordant inside. Adele had all the trappings of happiness, every reason to feel fortunate, but to her shame, she didn't care much that her husband was going off to war. After all, the truth was that they were close to being strangers, intimate strangers, yes. But only just married, and she stopped for a moment, realizing that she wasn't sure, two years or more. She'd have to check her datebook. How silly of her not to keep track of such an important thing.

It was late in the morning, and she didn't have anywhere else to go. She decided to stop at the café in the store to have some coffee. By this time, she'd entirely forgotten about the china pattern.

It was nearly lunchtime when he first approached her table. In fact, it was exactly 11:43 A. M. on October 13, 1942. That was the date when everything changed.

The morning was flooding into her consciousness, and somewhat less quickly was reason. Mika shakily sat up in an alien bed, in an unfamiliar room, with no coherent idea how she got there. Her head was pounding without mercy, and her stomach churned with nausea, then fast and relentless on its heels came the fear — like a blanket covering everything.

She scrambled to her feet on trembling limbs and shakily tried to smooth herself out. This, in itself, was impossible. She seemed crumpled everywhere, as though she'd been in some sort of a tussle. Her long-sleeved rayon shirt looked like it had been squished up in a ball at some point, and her off-white linen pants didn't look much better.

Trying to force herself into a semblance of composure, she glanced around at her surroundings. If she weren't so upset, she might appreciate it. It was a large, paneled room with a high ceiling. The furniture had a rustic quality, light pine pieces, a dresser, and a nightstand. And there was a table of the same wood that looked perhaps like a desk. And she blinked, a bit taken aback — yes, four rather huge, white pillar candles, all still lit, stationed on wooden stands at different corners. Odd didn't quite cover it.

She turned toward the front of the room, just noticing the curtain at that end. She walked to it, pushing the lightweight drape aside, realizing that this was a sliding glass door leading onto a porch. Even from here, she could see outside the house, down a well-forested hill to a river. As she stood there taking in the scene, a peculiar familiarity washed over her, reminding her of something, and then she dismissed it. She was sure she'd never been here before.

She had no idea what was going on, what strangeness was occurring here at the house of James Clairmont, but what was clear was that she was getting out as quickly as her feet could take her. Her purse was sitting on top of the dresser. Picking it up, she fished out her car keys with fingers that still wanted to shake. But she stilled them. She must regain control.

She ran her hands through her dark hair but didn't bother to check her appearance. Quite silently, she opened the door to the room and glanced into the den. It was empty. That slowed down her pounding heart just a notch. Perhaps, there was some plausible explanation for everything, and she was being rude and highly inappropriate sneaking out this way. But her mind was highly unsuccessful in taking her emotions out of the mix — trapped, afraid, in danger — all of it boiling up in her like a geyser.

She clutched her purse beneath her arm and moved as fast as she could through the spacious den, reaching the front door without incident. As she flung it open, her heart painfully clutched in her chest. There he was, the author of all of this upset, standing in the driveway next to her car. She stood frozen, at a complete loss of what to do now. Then as if responding to that thought, he turned casually around, facing her with a smile.

Forcing herself into action, she stepped into the driveway and moved toward the car. She steeled her voice and pushed the fear out of it. "I'm going back to the hotel."

The smile faded just a fraction as another unreadable emotion drifted into his eyes. "Are you feeling better? You seemed ill last night."

Her hand was shaking as she nervously ran it through her hair again. "I don't remember last night."

Slowly he nodded as though, for some reason, that didn't surprise him, "Are you sure you feel up to driving back to town?"

She answered emphatically, "Yes, I just need to go."

And then he suddenly moved closer and reached out, softly brushing her cheek with the side of his hand. The unexpected contact startled her. It was so gentle, so passive. "We didn't get to talk as much as I wanted."

It felt like she was caught in a whirl of confusion. Nothing she was feeling fit into any sensible pattern. "I know. I just have to get back."

And then he moved a step away from her, his face resigned, "Of course, I'll call you later to see how you are."

Without acknowledgment, she opened the car door, climbing in shakily. Quite smoothly, he reached out and closed it behind her. As she pulled back onto the path leading out of the forest, she saw him in the mirror, quietly watching her. She turned onto the main road, mentally re-tracking her steps of the night before. She was at least a good mile away from his house when she started to cry uncontrollably.

"Devon Carlyle"

She sat there, looking up at him foolishly. His hand was extended, and the only polite thing she could think to do was to shake it. "I'm sorry, Mr. Carlyle. I'm afraid you have me confused with someone else."

He smiled in a very warm way. In fact, in a way, she couldn't remember ever being looked at before. "I don't know. I was told I was to meet a lovely young lady here at noon. Granted, I'm a bit early, but you do seem to fit the bill."

She was sure she must have blushed. He was flirting with her, and in minutes, it would end. She glanced up at him with a wry sort of smile. "Well, my name is Adele St. Clair, does that sound familiar?"

His eyes still twinkled, but his mouth bent down in a slight grimace. Of course, now he'd realized his mistake. "No, I'm afraid it does not. The lady in question's name was Myers, and as I'm now remembering, a blond, not a redhead."

She nodded, "Well, Mr. Carlyle, I haven't seen anyone of that description, but I must admit I haven't been looking either."

He was still smiling, evidently somewhat pleased with her company. "Yes, to my shame, I have to admit it was sort of an arranged meeting. But I'm beginning to get the distinct impression I've been set up. A friend of mine who arranged this, well, he has a peculiar sense of humor."

She shrugged, glancing at the clock on the wall that had just made noon. "You might want to give her a bit more time."

He eyed her oddly, making her feel like she was being appraised. It was not unpleasant, although she was certain it was less than proper on some level. "Would it be terribly presumptuous Miss St. Clair if I waited here with you?"

She decided that propriety demanded she end this exchange. So somewhat reluctantly, she explained, "Well, it is actually Mrs. St. Clair, and I was only planning to be here a few minutes to have a cup of coffee."

He nodded oddly, unphased by her revelation, "Mrs., is it? So, your husband lets you go out and mingle with the riff-raff like me."

She laughed at his reference to himself. Whatever he claimed, Mr. Devon Carlyle was well-dressed in a nice grey suit, well-groomed, and actually quite handsome. Riff-raff was not the first description that came to mind, "My husband is a major in the army. He's just left to return to Europe."

"I see. Well, then, to support the war effort, perhaps I should keep his lovely wife company and safe from any other riff-raff." Again, she laughed. He was entertaining. She should say no, but she didn't want to. He'd managed to distract her in these few moments in a way she hadn't been for some time.

She indicated the chair, "If you wish, but if your appointment shows up, wouldn't she be upset to find us together?"

He shrugged, "Maybe she will." His eyes were a blue color, and they were sparkling again. It made her feel the slightest bit uneasy, as though she were traveling in a direction she shouldn't be.

She glanced away from him, "I don't know how long I'm going to stay."

He smiled, undaunted by much of anything, "Well, why don't we just see where things take us?" For the first time, it drifted into her consciousness that he had a slight accent, almost Scottish, she thought.

It was nearly ten when Mika arrived back at the hotel. She sat on the bed for some time, trying to figure out what had happened and what she should do about it. But nothing came clearly, and she was in much too panicked a state to sort through the incoherent images floating around in her mind. So instead, she opted to sleep to try to sand away the rough edges from the night before.

The sleep that came was deep and untroubled, filled with calmness.

There was a room toward the front of the house off the den. It wasn't a particularly large room, but it did have a set of built-in bookshelves on one wall, so he'd designated it as a kind of study. Here, he'd set up a computer and an array of old books he'd collected over his lifetime — some for pleasure, most for information's sake. And there was a blank wall between the bookshelves, where he'd deliberately never placed anything until now. Earlier this morning, not so long after he'd watched Mika drive away in her rental car, he'd hung the Raybourne.

He sipped his coffee and sat in his rather large office chair in the corner of the room, looking at the painting. Its history was sketchy. He did know that some years ago it had belonged to his great-uncle and was moved around quite a bit, from New York to Florida, then up again to Maryland, before it left the family. He'd never actually laid eyes on the original — that was until last night.

Things hadn't gone as he hoped. Everything had turned into a bit of a fiasco. He didn't know what he'd expected. But the attack that was launched on Mika Devalieur had stunned even him. Of course, it made sense that she would attract the low ones gathered in the area. She was raw, unprotected, clueless as to everything, and, of course, entirely too vulnerable.

That surprised him. The emotional upheavals of her life had eroded her to a degree that she was utterly defenseless against these sorts of spiritual aggressions.

He'd actually considered keeping her here at the house until he could build up her resistance a bit, but that plan had flown out the window when she'd walked out of his door this morning with complete primal horror written in her eyes. It was a complicated combination to be so unprotected yet so sensitive.

His gaze wandered back to the painting, away from the figure and to the skull on the table. It was clever of him to place his dominant symbols in such a fashion to adeptly contain what was being held.

Duality

It was nearly three in the afternoon when Mika awoke. Her head throbbed, but she quickly realized that she hadn't eaten all day. She felt a little better outside of the hunger factor but was wholly indecisive about what to do now. It occurred to her that perhaps she should check out today and drive to another city for the rest of the week. She was interested in the Virginia Beach area, or she could just go further into the mountains. There were options. It might be best to leave the painting and all that went with it behind her.

She was digging through her suitcase to gather fresh clothes for a shower when her cell phone jarringly rang.

"Hello."

"Mika, good, you made it back in one piece. You had me concerned."

Her heart started hammering nervously at the sound of his voice. "James," she murmured.

"You didn't think I was going to abandon you just yet, did you? After all, I'm the reason you're here."

"Actually, my grandmother's the reason I'm here." she sank onto the bed, caught completely off-guard. She hadn't even begun to consider how she should deal with him.

There seemed to be hesitation. "True, so, are you feeling any better? Did you get any rest?"

She glanced at the bed behind her, feeling strangely bothered that he would ask. Chaotic images of another bed and sensations of him touching her arms, her face, elusively tried to creep in. "Yes, I slept for a while. I was just going to get into the shower." Why had she told him that, feeling oddly exposed with him?

"Well, then, I'll get to my point. I want to take you out to dinner. There's a very nice restaurant on the mall not far from you. We could walk there."

"Um, to be honest, I don't know what kind of company I'd be tonight."

Another pause, but then he continued, seeming undaunted. "Well, you have to eat, and I would very much like to spend more time with you, bad company or not. What do you say?" Undeniably she was torn, caught up in a mishmash of emotions, curious about him, his connection to the painting but oddly fearful in other ways. He did make it sound so inviting, so safe now. But last night— what exactly happened to her last night? "Still there?"

"Yes," she said quietly, "just thinking."

"You know, you were courageous to come out here to Virginia. Don't leave without what you came for."

"I'm not exactly sure what that is anymore."

"I'll meet you downstairs about four-thirty. We'll make it an early dinner in case you'd like me to show you around town later. What do you say?"

What odd undercurrents. He was gentle with her, tactful, yet amazingly persistent. "All right," she wasn't sure why she gave in, but she did.

"Excellent, and Mika, I'm looking forward to seeing you again."

She didn't reply, but the phone clicked as he hung up. She lay back on the bed, feeling more than a bit disoriented. Her instincts were twisted in confusion. The duality confounded her. She was drawn yet filled with anxiety at the same time. What in the world could she do with that?

After a long, leisurely lunch, they'd gone for a stroll in the area and then had coffee in an outdoor café near the French Quarter. It was an amazingly lovely afternoon. For several hours, Adele had forgotten everything, her life, her husband, her future. She'd become a young, carefree woman again, unencumbered by the choices she'd made.

Devon Carlyle was a charming young man, well-traveled, and as he explained to her an aspiring collector of antiques. He walked with a cane due to a leg injury, although it didn't seem overly apparent from her vantage point. That was the reason he wasn't in the service. And she'd discovered that he was not married and did not intend to be in the foreseeable future. Adele was utterly determined that she would not take him too seriously in any respect and that she would never see him again after today. At the end of the afternoon, she'd extended her gloved hand to him in a handshake of farewell. He'd eyed her curiously with a twinkle in his green eyes, pulling her forward by that gloved hand and planting a very light kiss on her cheek. Then he walked away.

She didn't remember giving him her address, but one week later to the day, she received her first letter from him.

Mika had met her husband at a party at the house of another professor at the University. It was a Christmas party, and she had recently joined the faculty. At this point, she was conscious of appearances and made every effort to attend such gatherings, regardless of how uncomfortable she felt at them.

But this party was particularly significant. She remembered it clearly for two reasons: she'd just made thirty and met a man she could envision marrying.

At that point, in some very tangible ways, she was resigned to the fact that she would never marry. She'd seen marriage. She'd seen it with her mother three times, and it wasn't something she coveted by any stretch of the imagination.

But then she met a young, blondish lawyer who would turn such declarations on their head. At that particular juncture in his career, he was on a crusade against a group of local factories polluting the Mississippi River. It was a class-action suit, and he was fiery and hungry. He was going to change the world, and it was a bandwagon that she was more than happy to hop aboard.

There was something terribly romantic about an idealist, a crusader, a well-dressed, well-paid rebel. In fact, it was downright intoxicating. Theirs was a pretty quick engagement, four months. It took six more before his idealism burned out and settled into realism, then pragmatism. It didn't take long to figure out that they wouldn't change the world, less time for him than for her. And over seven more years, they slowly acknowledged that the glue that brought them together had faded.

These reflections took hold as she dressed to meet James Clairmont. She dressed rather casually, at least by her standards, in a silky red blouse over a denim skirt. The shower had helped, helped settle her nerves a bit. And her logical mind had talked her out of anything else nagging at her. James would provide whatever pieces of the night before that had yet to come together, and everything would make sense. Then she would go home and begin again.

At a little after four-thirty, she wandered down into the lobby of the Omni hotel. This room, bordering on the size of a small stadium, was quite impressive and airy, with a glass ceiling that stretched up at least four to five floors. It had the atmosphere of a botanical garden with its great glass windows, see-through ceiling, and strategically placed foliage. As she walked inward, she spotted him sitting amongst a collection of chairs on one side of the room.

She slowly strolled across the expansive lobby toward him as he stood up. He greeted her with a warm smile, "Well, you look refreshed."

He was dressed rather casually in khaki pants with an off-white sweater. She had noticed the early autumn weather here was much chillier than back home. "I feel better but hungry. I haven't managed to find time to eat much today."

He indicated a set of glass doors leading out into the outdoor mall. "Then let's be on our way. Do you like Italian food?"

She nodded, feeling quite reassured by his manner, "That's fine." All of the upset earlier must have been an overreaction on her part, her nerves simply overwrought from the journey. Surely, there was nothing to worry about.

"Good, it's not far," was his reply.

As James and Mika walked across the cobblestone bricks of the Charlottesville outdoor mall, he couldn't help but recall his first time here. He had been twenty years old. He remembered this clearly as it was a landmark in what he liked to refer to as his life's work. He and his uncle were traveling, visiting areas of the country of interest, at least what his uncle deemed were of interest. At the time, this small college town in Virginia seemed like an odd choice, but Gideon Reynolds, his mother's eldest brother, had his reasons for what he did, and questioning him about those reasons was often ill-advised. The information he gave out was sparse and calculatingly well-timed.

Looking back, it was a cold day, closer to December than this evening. It was morning too. He recalled pulling his blue jean jacket more tightly around himself. He hadn't anticipated the cold. Of course, he'd been living in Florida, where the weather tended to be much warmer.

Gideon, as he called his uncle, was in his fifties at the time — never having been married and living abroad most of his life. As they walked slowly down the mall, meandering without direction, he remembered Gideon stopping suddenly at a set of wrought-iron benches somewhere in the middle of the mall. His uncle sat down and looked up at him with his very dark blue eyes and unshaven face with an air of expectancy.

"What?" He remembered murmuring, perhaps just edged with a slight tinge of frustration that his uncle's opacity seemed to elicit in him.

There was a frown as if to say this was too obvious a question. "This place is a dichotomy. Both sides dwell here. Now it's time to put into practice what you are."

James wasn't quite as clueless as perhaps he had let on. By then, he had known for some time that he did not see the world as most did. But it was only recently that James discovered that this particular talent was a family trait in the blood. As requested, he settled next to his uncle and allowed his eyes to wander the mall.

As he did so, his vision shifted a bit, and he slowly began to see an ugly red glow blanketing much of the area. It was disturbing, thick, and oozing like blood. The sight was chilling, although, admittedly, it was not the first time he'd witnessed such a phenomenon.

"I thought you said it was mixed," he muttered.

"It is," Gideon grumbled with obvious irritation in his voice. James also felt agitated, but that was normal when one was close to such negativity. "Evidently, something happened here recently to tip the scales."

James reluctantly allowed himself to look further. He knew that whatever he saw now would not be good and would be extreme enough to create quite a concentration of negative energy.

The event itself came to him in fragments. But it was fresh, perhaps as recent as only days earlier — groups of teenagers wandering the mall. There were several groups, but clearly, one stirred to violence.

He swallowed with a dry throat, forcing himself to continue to watch. Even broken, it was graphic — an attack, brutal, several girls violently raped, repeatedly. It was so horrendous for him to see that he began to withdraw from the vision. "No, wait," his uncle insisted. "What else?"

James, somewhat angry at being forced to endure this, made himself move back a level to see what was beyond. Outside the group of attackers, there were the other creatures, quite a number, draining energy from the event. Some were not very evolved, and others were more so. Even two of the boys themselves were drainers. He could see the energy being pulled out of the girls as they were attacked sexually. Their terror and upset made them easy prey. "There were so many of them, so many drainers."

"I know. Sorry to make you see that." His uncle answered with concern in his voice.

"It seemed," James hesitated, unsure what he wanted to say, "I don't know."

"Orchestrated?"

"Yes," That was exactly what he was feeling, "planned somehow by the creatures."

He nodded, "Yes, we call them the low ones. They're strong here right now. They influence far too much."

Painful Recollections

She reminded him of France. And that thought in itself he found unusual. Her hair was about shoulder length but wavy, dark brown. And her eyes were wide and dark but flecked with a generous amount of amber. Perhaps, it was her demeanor. She had a gracious and delicate way of speaking, strong surely, but not what he'd call an aggressive woman. And strangely, all of this reminded him of France, where he'd spent his honeymoon many years ago. In a way, there was a decided enchantment to Mika, a veiled, mysterious quality that he did not remember encountering in many people he'd met during his lifetime

"Well, how do you like it?" he inquired.

Her brown eyes were drawn back to him. She'd been distracted, staring out the large plate glass window near them and watching the pedestrians passing by. She frowned, "Sorry, what did you say?"

He smiled. He was enjoying himself, although he had not intended to do so. He had objectives, objectives that might cause some to label him calculating or cold, and usually, such objectives superseded everything. But something was creeping into this encounter, a relaxed familiarity he hadn't anticipated. "I was wondering how you liked the restaurant."

"Oh," she smiled in a way that seemed quite natural to him, as though he knew that she hadn't expected to at all, "I like it. It's very atmospheric."

He nodded, "But the food is not up to your usual standards?"

Again, the lovely smile made him feel like she was somehow remarkably vulnerable. The plate of pasta before her was largely untouched. She glanced down, twirling her fork and shaking her head, "No, it's fine. Strange, I'm hungry but not also."

"You know, you should eat. You'll feel better."

And then she glanced up at him again with a bit of hesitancy, perhaps just a shadow of fear. He didn't need to read her to know she was thinking of the night before, fearing possibly all sorts of things.

Succinctly, he decided it was best to get this out of the way as quickly as possible. "Why don't you drink some of your wine Mika, and then tell me what you want to know."

Her eyes widened at his directness. Surprisingly, she did as he asked and took several sips of the glass of Chianti before her. He leaned back in his chair, quietly waiting for her to start in her own time, and finally, she spoke. And at that moment, he reaffirmed his original estimation that he'd formed somewhere during their initial conversations of how much he truly enjoyed the sound of her voice. "Last night, what happened disturbed me greatly."

Somewhere during the time she'd begun speaking, he'd picked up his glass of wine, sipped it, and begun formulating some very soothing answers to the questions he knew were coming. "I know. You left very upset this morning," he offered.

She seemed a little shaken by that. He wondered what she'd expected. "I wasn't trying to be rude."

"It never crossed my mind that you were," he answered smoothly.

"Well, frankly, I still have no idea what happened, but I did come away with some very odd impressions."

"What sort of impressions?" he asked quietly.

Her eyes went down to the plate before her, and again, she started to twirl her fork nervously in her fettuccine. He extended his hand and softly placed it on her wrist to still her. Her eyes met his. "It's all right," he said, "just tell me."

Slowly, she deliberately retracted her hand from the contact. "I remember sitting with you in the den talking."

"Yes, I thought we would be doing quite a bit more talking last evening."

"That's why I came here, to Virginia, for answers, I suppose. I could have sent the painting without coming, but there were things I wanted to understand."

"About the painting?"

She hesitated, then continued, "Yes, and then I remember standing up and feeling sick, I mean dizzy."

"You fainted."

She looked at him with quite a penetrative stare that told him she questioned that event. "I have to tell you. I'm not the sort to faint, James. I can't remember ever having fainted in my whole life."

It made him want to smile, her defensiveness. Evidently, she took this as some sign of weakness. "You've been under a lot of stress lately. Perhaps, it all caught up with you."

She glanced away abruptly, focusing away from him. The description stubborn floated across his mind. She was reluctant to accept this explanation. "I suppose that could be it, and the flight here. But it's just unlike me."

"Stress is a funny thing. It can elicit unfamiliar reactions in people."

And then again, moods shifting, she was looking at him pointedly, "Then what happened?"

He found it quite captivating, in a way, these fluctuations in attitude. He imagined she was a water sign, emotions swirling and running so profoundly deep. Quite flatly, trying not to overly alarm her, he explained, "I caught you when you fainted. Then I went and laid you down on the bed."

"The bed?" It was no use. Flashes of alarm were passing across her features, much as she tried to suppress them.

"My bedroom Mika was the closest one available."

"The one with all the candles?"

"Hmmm," he nodded again, sipping his wine just to buy time. "My mother was a big fan of candles. I'm afraid I've carried on with it."

"My grandmother liked candles," she murmured.

"Yes, they are very atmospheric and creative in a way. "

Again, he waited, not wanting to explore this particular subject any more deeply than she wanted to take it. She sighed heavily, "I remember other things, impressions. I remember feeling your hands on me."

He could read her concern at mentioning this fact. It was palpable. So, he did his best to reassure her. "I checked on you several times, Mika. You were restless in your sleep, frantic at times. I touched your arms and your face, trying to calm you. I'm sorry if that alarmed you."

"I-I just didn't understand what was going on."

And then he met her gaze quite directly, feeling it was time to get this little issue out of the way. "Look, I realize we don't know each other well, but I'm not the sort of man to take advantage of an unconscious woman."

She hesitated, taken aback by this abrupt declaration, "I didn't mean to suggest." She hesitated, "but you must understand why all this would seem unusual at the least and—" she seemed genuinely debating whether or not to go on. "I remember something else."

"What's that?" he asked calmly.

She was trying to contain it, but her voice trembled slightly as she spoke. "I remember hands pulling at me, at my clothes — trying to touch me, and cold, a terrible coldness." The last part was nearly a whisper.

He nodded, trying to cover his surprise at the details she recalled, "You were thrashing quite a bit in your sleep, Mika. I'm quite sure it was some sort of fevered dream."

She waited, staring at him for a moment, perhaps trying to discern the truth, then said softly, "I suppose." It seemed, for now anyway, she was willing to accept this rendition of events.

Feeling a bit on more level ground, he lightly touched her hand, and she looked up at him. "So, how about eating, and I'll show you around the city a bit?"

She smiled tentatively. As he leaned back in the chair, James took a moment to truly look at her. What was clear was that last night had drained her quite a bit. He could tell how low her energy was from the aura he could see around her, diminished by the attack the night before. But what was also clear was that it wasn't the first time. The tell-tale glow of yellow around her heart area told him she'd been drained of energy before and was still feeling its influence.

"You're not acting yourself."

She'd heard the remark, but it didn't penetrate much, irritate, yes, but truly be comprehended? Not for some years yet. She was tired and didn't want complications. She smiled blandly at her grandmother. Mika had taken her out to lunch late one Saturday afternoon. She had meant to do it more often, but her marriage had allowed it to fall by the wayside. "What do you mean?" She attempted a complacent smile. Lately, she'd found herself in the role of the placater. It was an unexpected part for her to play, but one she had slipped into perhaps while she was unaware.

Her grandmother had eyed her with a shrewd expression that could peel back any layers of façade she cared to attire herself with. "You just seem different, Mika. I don't know, not nearly as confident."

She frowned and took a sip of her iced tea. The last thing she wanted today was to be dissected. She had envisioned a nice, calm, relaxing lunch with the one woman who had always accepted her for what she was. And now that woman was telling her that she was not acting as she should. Again, she attempted a smile meant to return the mood to a level of superficiality. "Well, you know how marriage is, Gran, the land of compromises."

Adele St. Clair frowned explicitly at that remark. "Unfortunately, I know it can be my dear. But I admit I hoped it wouldn't be so for you."

Mika laughed, although she felt an unexpected heaviness in her heart at that admission from the older woman. "It's not so bad. It's just Nathan leads a complicated life, and things sort of revolve around that."

Once more, the frown, but this time added with a dash of sternness, "And what about you? When do things get to revolve around you?"

She shrugged, not allowing that question to penetrate either. In fact, it was some years before she allowed herself to contemplate such matters seriously. At that point, she was only two years into her marriage. It would be some time yet before all hope began to permanently fall away.

"Hey, where are you?"

Abruptly, she pulled herself back to the present. She had no idea why lately she so often drifted into painful recollections. Perhaps, it was the loss of her grandmother. She did enormously regret the time she didn't spend with her while she was with Nathan. But they were quite inseparable in the last year of Adele's life. Maybe in some small way, that made up for her prior neglect.

"I don't know, lost in thought."

"Well, you're missing all this wonderful scenery. Now, don't blink, or it might be over," he said somewhat whimsically.

They had walked the mall a bit after dinner, and then James had insisted he take her for a drive near the UVA campus. She had to admit it was impressive. Fortunately, dusk hadn't quite settled in so she could easily make out the sprawling grounds of the college. "You sound like you don't like it around here."

He murmured lightly, "I suppose my feelings are mixed. Perhaps, I've just been here too long."

"I can't imagine feeling that way about New Orleans," she commented. "Even with all the changes it's been through, I can't picture myself elsewhere."

"Then you must belong there. You're lucky you realize that. Most people never find that place they belong." She glanced over at his profile. There had been the slightest tinge of sadness in his voice, but then again, it might have been her imagination. All evening he'd been calm, soothing, and quite friendly. But she couldn't shake the impression that there was something else just beneath the surface of this pleasantry, something quite exacting.

"So, coffee wouldn't be out of the question?"

"No, that would be nice."

"I know a nice coffee house on the other side of town. It will allow you to see the rest of the city, although it's just largely commercial, not as scenic as downtown."

"It sounds fine," her voice drifted off. She felt strange and relaxed, regardless of the divergent vibes she'd picked up from James. It was odd also. They had yet to talk about the painting or her grandmother all evening. After all, wasn't that what this trip was all about in the first place?

Correspondences

They would meet in the park, Audubon Park, on Tuesday afternoons. It took three, perhaps four letters, from Devon Carlyle before Adele consented to do so. The first letter was entirely unexpected. He didn't even write his name on the envelope, only his address, so she had no idea who was writing her. The truth was that it came as somewhat of a shock when she first opened it.

October 23, 1943
Dear Mrs. St. Clair,

I can imagine that you are not expecting to hear from me. But I have to confess since our afternoon some weeks back, I have not been able to get you out of my mind. It is rare when one meets, and I am sure you will laugh at me at this reference, but forgive my romanticism, a kindred spirit.

I felt from our first acquaintance that you were indeed a person I could talk with freely and, oddly enough, who would understand me.

I know it is quite bold, but I must ask if there is any possible way that we could meet again, just for a little while. I feel it is so very essential that I see you once more.

Yours Sincerely,
Devon Carlyle

After receiving the letter, she felt no compunction and hesitation in dealing with the situation swiftly and irrevocably.

October 23, 1943
Dear Mr. Carlyle,

I received your letter and within it your request. Our last meeting, while very pleasant, was merely by chance. Another would be a different matter and perfectly out of the question. As I made it clear to you, I am married and have no wish to bring any embarrassment to my husband or family with behavior that might be misinterpreted.

All My Best,
Adele St. Clair

She mailed the letter the same day that his mail arrived. That she felt certain was the end of the matter and resolved to put it entirely out of her mind. This inflexible resolve lasted perhaps for the rest of the day. That night the dreams began – disturbing dreams, but certainly not what one might call nightmares. They were dreams of another land, green and rich with ornate ruins of medieval castles marking the landscape. She was there with Devon Carlyle walking together, hand in hand, down a green slope with the bluest sky she'd ever seen overhead.

The following letter arrived a week later to the day.

October 29, 1943
Dear Mrs. St. Clair,

After receiving your last letter, I am certain you had no expectation of hearing from me again. And quite frankly, I had no expectation of writing. But something very strange has occurred. Several nights ago, I began to have some very unusual dreams, dreams that centered around you. Of course, you might consider them simply a product of some fancy that I am nurturing for you. If that were merely their nature, I would keep this to myself. However, what is particularly disturbing to me is your state of distress in these dreams. You appear always to be quite troubled and even fearful. Although I am not a believer in such visionary sciences, they are concerning enough to make me write again so that I can assure myself that all is well with you, Adele. Please confirm your well-being for me. And I assure you, I will not bother you again.

Regards,
Devon Carlyle

October 31, 1943
Dear Mr. Carlyle,

I fear I was too abrupt with you in my last letter. I appreciate your concern for my well-being. There are stresses for everyone during wartime. Of course, I have great anxiety about my husband. Curiously, I have to confess my dreams have also been disturbed lately. I thank you for your concern.

Kind Regards,
Adele St. Clair

Another week passed, and Adele felt sure that she had heard the last of Devon Carlyle, and that realization left her with a heaviness in her heart that was as inexplicable as it was unexpected. And then, quite to her astonishment, there was another correspondence.

November 19, 1943
Adele,

I ask again. Can we meet? Please send me a quick reply, or I will take your silence as a negative response.

Devon

Two days later, she put pen to paper again,

November 21, 1943
Dear Devon,

Forgive me. It's not possible.

Adele

For the remainder of November, there was silence, silence that began to fester like an unattended wound. There was word that George would have his holiday leave at the beginning of the year. There was too much going on for him to come home for Christmas. It now struck her as odd, in a way that had never before, the occasional letters she would get from George. They were so very abrupt and dry. He never spoke of his affection for her in them or even how he missed her, just surreptitiously of his life, only what he was experiencing in a very peripheral manner. It left her feeling hollow, especially now after she'd corresponded with Devon.

And the dreams continued, most recollections of these she forced herself to forget in the daylight hours. It was only in the darkness when she was tormented.

Early in December, on a whim, she sent Devon a Christmas card. There wasn't much to it, just a short note saying,

I hope your holidays are lovely.

Two days later, another envelope arrived. By now, she quickly identified his script, although he did not ever sign his name.

December 5, 1943
Adele,

On Tuesday, I'll be walking near St. Andrew's church at the corner of Audubon Park. I'll be there after 2:00 P.M.

Devon

For some time, she simply stared at the note, transfixed. It was not possible that she could do this. But somehow, deep inside, she knew that she still would.

It was a quaint place, very atmospheric with its dark colors, wooden tables, and a leather sofa and chairs positioned in front of a fireplace that was lit tonight. New Orleans did not lack atmospheric coffee shops, but even Mika had to admit that this was an exceptionally comfortable one.

As they settled into a corner table, she couldn't resist throwing out the old line, "So, do you come here often?"

James glanced up at her with a sparkle of amusement in his eyes. He'd just settled into his chair, so her comment caught him off-guard. "Occasionally, I'd say. It has its charm."

She let her eyes flicker across their surroundings. There were a few other customers, but it wasn't what one would call packed by any standard. But she preferred it that way. Crowds tended to make her uncomfortable, always had. Again, she focused on the man before her. The uneasiness she'd felt earlier in the evening had all but dissipated. She had to admit, even to herself, that she was enjoying his company. She couldn't remember the last time she'd spent an evening with such an attractive and attentive man. "It's a nice place." She sipped her coffee and relaxed even further.

"I'm glad you like it. So, I gather you're a person who needs atmosphere."

She smiled freely, "Why would you say that?"

"I have a sense of these things. You strike me as the creative type, and creative people need atmosphere like the rest of us need food."

She laughed, "Well, I don't know if I'd call myself creative. I'm drawn to creative things, people," and then she shrugged, "paintings."

He nodded, immediately catching onto her train of thought. "The Raybourne, it was very difficult for you to give it up."

"Yes, very difficult, I don't know, somehow it felt very tied to my grandmother, a link to her. I know that sounds strange, but I clung to that. I don't have many things or people in my life right now that I feel connected to."

He leaned back a bit in his chair, sort of strumming his fingers on the table. "So, the ex-husband, there is no friendship still there?"

Her eyes shot to his face, feeling slightly startled at the inquiry. The question surprised her, its content and pointed delivery. "No, we didn't part on amicable terms."

"I'm sorry. I suppose I'm getting too personal," he said smoothly. It made Mika feel as though she was overreacting. She was used to being so defensive with people, expecting ulterior motives from everyone, probably a by-product of her unstable upbringing.

"Yes, I mean, I don't know. I think maybe I'm still too sensitive about it all."

"These emotional matters often take a long time to heal, often much longer than we'd like," he offered.

He had that very curious dichotomy of simultaneously making her feel at ease and yet nervous. "It's just that things deteriorated between us in an unexpected way."

He took a sip from his still steaming mug, then focused on her face again with an intense expression that gave her the strange feeling that he was looking for something in particular. "How so?" he asked, "or am I prying again?"

She shook her head, "Maybe, prying a bit, I just don't usually talk about it much, not even to my grandmother. In some ways," she laughed, "many ways, she subbed for my real mother. So, there were expectations there," she glanced away, now feeling vulnerable for talking so much. She felt his hand softly touch hers, and again, she looked back at him.

"I find you intriguing, Mika. So, I can't help digging a bit to get to know you better." His touch sent a definitive sensation through her. And at this moment, she acknowledged how attracted she was to this man.

She slowly removed her hand, wrapping it around her coffee mug in an attempt to collect her thoughts. "Umm, let's see. Nathan was, how can I say it, surprised by the separation. I don't know why, but he didn't see it coming. He thought I would just stay, even though—" And then she stopped. How could she explain this to an almost total stranger when it was so difficult for her to understand?

"Even though you were unhappy."

"Yes, I guess, even though I was unhappy," she repeated softly. "At first, he became very hurt, and then antagonistic when he realized there wouldn't be a reconciliation." She shrugged, "I don't know. I'd seen him turn on other people before, in that very vitriolic way, but I never thought he would turn on me like that—"

He nodded as though taking time to consider her words. "But he did."

"Yes," she smiled grimly, "it got ugly and painful. I would have preferred to end things quickly, calmly. But he decided he wanted to hurt me as much as possible."

His face reflected compassion at her words and then something else, surprising. A flicker of anger, perhaps disdain, crossed his features directed toward, she had no doubt, her ex-husband. "I'm sorry you had to go through that, Mika." He remarked in a caring but oddly stern voice. She felt that he was sincere, although, in truth, she had nothing concrete to base that opinion on.

She laughed shortly, trying to break the intensity. "I'm surprised I'm talking about this at all. It's not really what I intended."

Now smiling, he sipped his coffee again, back to his charming but perfectly natural self. "And what did you intend, Dominique Devalieur?"

"I really want to know why my grandmother left her most treasured painting to you."

He paused for a moment as though formulating his response carefully. "Well, there's a long and a short answer to that. So, I'll start with a question for you. Do you know how the painting came into your grandmother's possession?"

She considered that for a moment and then shook her head, "Not really, she had it before I was born, and my mother has no idea either. I asked her once."

"Did you ever ask your grandmother?"

"Yes, as a matter of fact, I did, but she didn't ever answer me, not in a direct way."

"What did she say?"

"I remember that she said it was a gift. That was all. But she never put the painting out on display in the house. It was always kept away, in a secret room."

He commented slowly, "That makes sense."

She leaned forward a bit. Her interest piqued, "It does? How so?"

"Well, the short answer is that it was put into your grandmother's hands, more for safekeeping than anything else."

"Safekeeping? What does that mean? You're not saying that there was something criminal involved."

He shook his head, but his dark blue eyes seemed focused elsewhere, somewhere in the past, quite beyond the two of them. "No, I wouldn't suggest that at all."

"So, do you know where she got the painting?"

"Yes, I do, actually, from a great uncle of mine by the name of Devon Carlyle."

Gambling

dele had no idea what to expect from this meeting. More than that, she had no idea why she'd kept the appointment at all. She should be concentrating on the holidays, on various family gatherings that were to take place, and then after that on George coming home. She'd received a card from him just the day before, with a quick little note written on it.

Darling,

Wish I was enjoying the holidays with you

I am looking forward to the New Year and seeing you.

Much Love,

George

On reflection, it was one of the warmer correspondences that she'd ever received from him, with the exception of before they were married. In a way, it felt as though he were throwing her a lifeline. Perhaps, they would be happy together. Perhaps, she should not go today and see Devon Carlyle. What good could come of it? A friendship, she supposed, but she had women friends. And those relationships were much more acceptable.

She took the streetcar to uptown New Orleans, getting off on St. Charles Avenue. She could have gotten off at a closer stop, but she wanted to stroll a bit, to think. After a while, she could see St. Andrew's church down the street. That was where he'd said that he would be. Slowing down, she walked a bit past it. Then suddenly, she spotted him sitting on a low wall on the east side of the church. From where she was, she could see that he was dressed in a suit, a light grey tweed. Her gloved hands nervously fingered her handbag as she contemplated leaving before he caught sight of her, but it was too late. He'd spotted her, and a broad smile crossed his lightly tanned face. As he moved in her direction, she felt keenly as though a door was somehow closing behind her.

Mika wore a curious look on her face that he found immensely appealing. "Did you know him?"

He shook his head. "No," that was the truth, although there were some things he'd said tonight that he would classify as convenient fabrications. He was, however, very familiar with the name Devon Carlyle and had seen photos.

"So, are you sure he gave the painting to my grandmother?"

He nodded, trying to be truthful without alluding too much to the real truth beneath the tip of the iceberg. There were truths, and there were truths Uncle Gideon used to tell him. And he felt there was no need to burden Ms. Devalieur with things she wasn't yet equipped to handle. "Yes, the Raybourne was given to Devon Carlyle by its previous owner, William Sandstone. From what I understand, he was from Boston, a rather wealthy entrepreneur."

"Really? I wonder why he would part with such a valuable piece of art."

He shrugged, allowing a flicker of a grin to cross his face. Better to let her think it was more superficial than it was. "From what I gather, it was won in a bet, a card game. Evidently, Mr. Carlyle was a bit of a gambler."

Her face seemed to blanch a bit at this. "You're kidding! He won it in a card game."

"Some men take their gambling very seriously, even rich ones."

The line of her very full mouth seemed to tighten a bit. She was angry. Perhaps, this made her feel that his family's claim to the painting was less than binding now. "Well, how did this gambler know my grandmother?" She had emphasized the word gambler in quite a distasteful way.

Again, he couldn't hold back a smile. He found her fluid shifts in mood quite fascinating. "That is unknown, only certain that they did know each other. And at some point, he placed the Raybourne into her keeping with the understanding that it was temporary."

"So why didn't he get it back?"

He met her gaze directly, trying to dispel some of the antagonism he sensed brewing within her at these revelations. "Although I feel that was his intention, it was clear he was unable to do so."

"Why?" Was her question, although her eyes were nearly accusing.

"Because he was killed in Scotland, some accident, I understand. He was quite young, just reached thirty, I believe."

Her eyes widened a bit. Good, that had diffused things somewhat. "That's terrible, but then how—" and her voice drifted off.

"The painting? Yes, I see where you're going. I don't know exactly how your grandmother knew to leave it to me. Perhaps an arrangement was made between them, but I can't say for sure."

"But you feel your family's claim to the painting is legitimate?"

He smiled at her. "Legitimate? Perhaps, perhaps not, but it was your grandmother's request."

That fact that apparently had been forgotten had some impact in its reappearance. "Yes, yes it was," she hesitated, murmuring, "and I don't suppose I have the right to question her judgment."

Again, he reassuringly touched her hand and could distinctly feel the flow of confusing and conflicting emotions moving through her. It was clear that Mika was emotionally on very shaky ground, and from what he could glean, had been so for some time. "I know this is difficult."

Her wide brown eyes met his with a distressed look. "I must seem very superficial to you, clinging so much to this."

"No, superficial is a word I can't imagine attaching to you under any circumstance."

She smiled a bit, looking a little embarrassed at the compliment. "My mother wanted the painting as well, but she wanted to sell it. Its value to me is very sentimental."

"I understand, and under other circumstances, I would give it back to you."

"Under other circumstances?"

He sighed deeply within, concerned for maybe the first time that he'd said too much. "Well, let's just say I think we're all better off if it stays in my keeping."

She eyed him with a distinct expression of curiosity. It surprised him. He almost felt her mind reaching out, the barest tentacles of energy. There was potential here, but she would have to be much stronger to develop it. "I don't understand what you mean by better off."

He felt as though he'd had quite the workout in being evasive. "I realize that, but for now, that's all I can say."

"But I'll be leaving soon. This may be my only opportunity to find out."

"Then we'll have to spend as much time together as possible while you're here."

Her already wide eyes seemed to widen a bit more, but she said nothing in response.

He'd deliberately parked outside the mall so they would have to walk a bit longer before they ended the evening. It wasn't particularly late, just after eight, but the night had fallen. The winter darkness was already beginning to encroach on the city, although it was only early Fall. But the seasons were shifting here, almost imperceptibly, but enough to signal a change for those watching.

She was quiet, caught deep within some secret place that was turbulent. He could feel this distinctly. He grabbed her hand, and she turned to him, startled by the contact. He indicated a wrought iron bench, not far away, for them to stop at for a moment.

Strange, but it had only just occurred to him as they sat that this was probably very near the spot that he and his Uncle Gideon had settled in so long ago. But tonight, fortunately, he felt nothing so ominous and threatening as he had that particular afternoon.

"What's troubling you?" he asked.

Her face reflected a bit of confusion, then something else. Yes, unfortunately, sadness, there was undeniable sadness here. It was a disturbing world for those who were sensitive yet had no comprehension of what they were feeling. The fluctuations of mood and emotions could quite potentially be maddening. "I don't know. I'm wondering why I came here at all. Right now, it feels sort of frivolous, reckless."

"Hmm, frivolous and reckless, all of that?"

She frowned at his flippancy, "I know it's silly, but in some odd way, I thought I would find something here, some answer that would help me, well, that would just help me. Thinking about it now and saying it out loud, it sounds ridiculous. There's nothing here for me. I think I should go home," she said bleakly. He could acutely feel the pain she was experiencing in her aimlessness. It reminded him of himself at a time that now feels like so very long ago.

Quite calmly, he entwined his arm in hers and grasped the hand he'd released only moments before. Instantly, he could sense how startled Mika was at the contact, but he did not allow that to deter him. He'd learned long ago when something or someone was stuck, it might take a mighty push to get them out.

Focusing intently, he allowed his energy to flow freely into her, not in a quiet, unobtrusive way, but a powerful wave. Quite sharply, he could feel her shock. Yes, there was no other word for it. She was so sensitive, even more so than he'd anticipated. Frightened as well, she tried to pull away, but he only tightened his grasp on her, not to be dissuaded from his purpose. "What are you doing?" she whispered raggedly.

"Trying to help you, Mika."

He allowed himself full perception, and his mind completely entered her consciousness. — Again, he felt the shock, then the fear. It was clear, too much, too soon. But this was what was needed to shake her up, shake her out of the prison she'd built for herself. And then, to his surprise, she abruptly yanked away from him. And on her feet, she took off running down the cobbled brick path at the mall's center. It took only moments before he decided to follow her.

"I wasn't sure if you'd be here."

They'd walked back into the park together, stopping at one of the many benches positioned along the pathway. Until then, little had been said, but now it was time to confront the awkward truths facing them. "I wasn't at all sure if I would either. I must admit your last letter — the abruptness of it — made me concerned for you, Devon. That's much of why I'm here, to see if you're all right."

He nodded quietly, staring off somewhere beyond her. She wasn't at all sure if he believed her or if she believed it. But it was a reasonable façade, an approximate of the truth to cloak herself in. "You're very perceptive," was his answer, but still, he wasn't focusing on her but rather somewhere beyond her. "In many respects, it's been a difficult time for me." And then he turned his attention to her directly and murmured. "Is your husband coming home for Christmas?" His eyes, that clear blue, weren't sparkling at her as they had the first time they'd met. They were intense, darkened in some way, she thought.

The question itself flustered her. Bringing him into this somehow magnified the feeling that this meeting was inappropriate. "Um, actually, he can't get away until the beginning of the year."

And then, very lightly, he put his hand over hers, and her nervousness magnified many times over. "That will be difficult for you, Adele, spending the holidays without your husband."

She looked down, quite overwhelmed. His hand felt so warm, but more than that. She answered, "I have family with me, mine and George's."

"But that's not quite the same as having your husband with you, is it?"

She swallowed, and then he removed his hand and tipped her face in his direction so she would meet his gaze. She was breathing deeply, that voice somewhere muffled in the back of her head speaking warnings of danger. "George isn't really like that."

"Like what?" he asked, ever so lightly tucking a wayward curl of her hair behind her ear. She had pulled it back into a low bun, but her thick, dark red hair rarely kept itself in check.

"He's not sentimental about things, like holidays."

And then he lightly brushed her cheek with his fingertips, and she closed her eyes, overwhelmed by the novel sensations flooding through her. "What are you like, Adele?"

Her eyes fluttered open just at the moment that he bent his head to kiss her. And thought became fractured into something entirely different.

A Selfless Man

Her skin was ablaze, a wild, mad tingling that was a hair's breadth away from being painful. In those quick moments when James rather forcefully took her hand, something impossible happened. It almost felt as though he'd poured fire into her. Instantaneously, her vision had swirled into a vivid spectrum of bright, painful colors.

She didn't remember pulling away from him. Her head pounded, and she was moving in a mad rush of panic. It was several seconds of running before she realized what she was doing, before she slowed. She had to regroup, had to figure out — some sort of seizure, maybe. But the ground below her felt unstable. She grabbed onto a small light post strategically placed along the mall for decorative purposes. She clung to it desperately, trying to still her breathing. But behind her, she heard footsteps catching up, and an instinctive fear took hold. James' hands came to rest on her shoulders. She could feel him, recognize him elementally, without even looking at his face. "No, no," she blurted out.

"It's all right. It's all right." He repeated in a soothing tone. He'd wrapped his arms around her while she still clung to the lamppost.

"I want to go back to my room," her voice sounded small and broken to her ears, drowned out by the roar of her fear.

His face was near her hair now, whispering in her ear. "No, no, Mika, you need to come with me." His voice was so soothing, calming to her panic. But that whisper, so quiet right now, told her definitively that he was the source of her panic.

She shook her head, still trembling with hysteria. "No, I need to go back to my room."

His hands moved up to her temples, softly massaging there. He murmured softly, "So stubborn." His touch was compelling, lulling. "Just relax," she heard before a sharp stab of pain went through her head and then complete blackness.

There was the recognition at once. Something they termed as *serch bythol* in the old country, kindred, everlasting love, although he did not know if he believed in it until now.

Devon Carlyle returned to his room on St. Charles Avenue that he'd leased nearly a month before. It was a single room in a boarding house. As he entered the front, he passed a parlor that functioned as a shared space. As he climbed the stairs, Adele's wide and confused eyes at their parting still stuck in his mind. If he were being fair, he would have left her to her life, to her husband, who wasn't the sentimental type. But he wasn't a particularly selfless man.

With distraction, he opened the door to his room. There were several stacks of books about. He was a collector, particularly of rare and valuable items. He sunk onto the single bed, his whole body humming with an altered awareness. It was her effect. He'd hardly expected to have this reaction to her. Then again, he'd hardly expected to stumble across her at all. He'd come to this city for a very different purpose, and Adele, well, Adele was somewhat of an accident.

His mind tripped back to that afternoon in the café when he'd first set eyes on her. He'd just been walking by, actually killing time that afternoon. An appointment to acquire an original text from the mystic Cagliostro had fallen through. The façade of a charming, depthless Scotsman was one he had developed. He'd been greatly disappointed and so was endeavoring to distract himself. It was best to throw people off his true nature.

As he wandered down Canal Street past a department store, he'd sensed it — an energy, a gentle but strong presence. He thought it might be a kinsman and meeting a familiar face at this point would be most welcome. But as he walked into the café, he realized who it was attached to, the lovely young woman in the lavender-colored dress. It was puzzling, to say the least. And then, he'd concocted a story so that he could approach her. At the very least, he had contrived to spend some time with a lovely lady.

He leaned back onto the bed, sighing deeply, wondering how exactly he'd let things become more complicated. Considering his dealings and his life, to begin an involvement with a married woman was more than madness.

He sat up and then moved to a table at the corner of the room. He pulled away the drape he'd placed across it. Each time he looked at it, a chill traversed him. It made him feel too deeply. He felt its textures and could smell the paint all around him in the drafty studio. His mind was pulled so strongly there. And as she turned, her unwound black hair spilled over the blue tapestry of her garment.

"Pull your hair back. It must be contained."

Fatigue marked her expression, but her long delicate hand did as he asked.

Devon pulled himself back from the image. He was a seer, had always been, as it was in his blood, and it was far too easy for him to be drawn in by such vibrations.

He allowed his mind to be pulled in another direction. He could see her. She was sitting on a massive bed in a closed room, her head bent, her slim hands covering her face. He loved her hair. It was so thick and dark, auburn, as though she came from back home in Scotland. It amazed him how already she pulled at his heart. She lifted her face. Tears marked it, still running down her cheeks.

He shouldn't have entered her life. But then again, he wasn't a selfless man.

The word kidnapping crossed his mind, but then he dismissed it.

It was for the best. If James hadn't made a proactive move, Mika Devalieur would have returned home, never knowing. He truly wished he were on as solid ground as he was trying to convince himself.

After she'd collapsed, it took some maneuvering for him to get her back to his car and then home again. He expected the acupressure technique he'd used to keep her unconscious through the night. But he wasn't sure. When it came to Mika, he wasn't sure at all.

Again, he'd laid her on the bed in his bedroom and lit the candles around her. He didn't sense that the attacks would be as strong tonight, unlike the first time. But he took what precautions he could. He used a binding energy as a protection surrounding her. And then he lay down beside her on the bed. He didn't feel comfortable at all about leaving her. His eyes silently watched the fan turn above them as he considered carefully what he was doing and why. In retrospect now, his actions seemed somewhat astonishing to him. It certainly wasn't as he planned. But then again, when did anything go as planned?

Christa was twenty-two when they met. She was a psychology major with long blond hair and eyes as blue as the clearest of skies. James was finishing his bachelor's degree at Michigan State University, a far cry from where he'd grown up, but as it was, he'd grown up everywhere.

When they met, he recognized that she would never be open to his other life. She was a kind-hearted, sensitive girl with boundaries that she would never step beyond. He knew it was a dangerous match, but something about her compelled him. And so, in his twenty-fifth year, he married Christa Morris. And he told his mother and the rest of the family that he was choosing a different path. Two months after their wedding, they left for graduate school in Montana.

He couldn't say he wasn't happy. Theirs was an idyllic, innocent sort of relationship. But he could say that he was not content. He knew now that it was possible to have sporadic happiness with no real peace attached to it. The problem certainly didn't seem to be his lovely young wife, although she was sensitive enough to feel his restlessness and, on some level, made insecure by it. During their brief five years of marriage, he worked hard to keep life on an even footing and reassure his bride. But it was difficult, as the visions did not go away but only became more potent and less controllable as he struggled to repress them.

It came as quite a shock when he first saw the drainers in action, the unevolved ones. With his Uncle Gideon, he'd sensed things, even saw them in a vague, distorted way, but never so concrete.

He'd been out at a night class late one evening. It was close to ten when he arrived, so he wasn't sure if Christa would be awake. Sometimes she'd wake up, and sometimes she wouldn't. Lately, her energy had been very low. So, he quietly let himself into the small brick house they'd rented. As he came inside, he saw a dim light coming from the den. Still trying to be quiet, he walked into the room.

Immediately, he saw his wife lying on the couch. But there was something else there also, blocking his vision. Something distorted, fuzzy, and black. He stood there, transfixed for some minutes, then finally allowed his vision to alter as he had been taught so very long ago.

The dark bestial-looking figure was bent over his wife with its hands, paws, whatever one might call them, on her. James felt frozen to the spot with fear with rage. And then it looked up at him, a horrible, distorted mouth salivating, and after making eye contact, bounded away, dissipating. Gently, he put his trembling hands on her, softly shaking her until she stirred. He could feel the energy draining out through his hands where he was touching her. She sat up, putting her arms around him. "I didn't hear you come in. I'm glad you woke me. I was having a nightmare."

He scooped her slight body into his arms and carried her into their bedroom. Later that night, he called his uncle.

"It's odd," he said, "These sorts of attacks aren't unusual. But it usually accompanies some deterioration. Is she losing energy, great amounts from somewhere else?" Of course, he knew at the time that the creature he'd seen was only symbolic, his mind's way of interpreting the powerfully negative nature of the thing he'd seen.

"I-I don't know." He ran his hand through his thick hair, still profoundly shaken by the whole episode.

"Hmm, that's right. You've left this behind, haven't you, my boy? Well, it appears it hasn't left you behind. It might do to keep your fingers in, just a bit, at least to keep your wife protected."

"What can I do?"

And then his re-entry had begun. He began to learn again, to study again, and then immerse himself in it. Christa did not protest his distraction this time. There was a definitive deterioration taking place in her. Within the year, she was diagnosed with heart disease brought on by a genetic condition that had gone unnoticed for years and had recently escalated inexplicably at an alarming rate. The following year was hell, one treatment after another failing until finally, she left him just three months after their fifth wedding anniversary. He'd thought in his grief-stricken mind that the spiritual attacks had brought this on. But his uncle assured him that this was not the case. They were not unrelated. The thing perhaps found an avenue of attack in her condition, but it was not responsible for it. That time with her, he'd always considered his innocent time when he had pretended that the world was something different than it truly was.

Buoyancy

Life had been different before her husband, Nathan. She had been different. In fact, to say quite succinctly that she'd been a different person wouldn't be entirely off the mark.

Her memories floated backward in an intangible way as though she were moving with them. Was it a memory or just a dream? Or had she died and slipped into some comforting state of oblivion?

The day was warm, not hot, but warm and overcast. She recognized what was around her. It was the campus at Loyola. She knew it because it was reassuringly familiar, the stone benches, the buildings. It spoke to her of that other, earlier time.

Thus, she decided that it must be a memory, perhaps one she'd forgotten. But her body at the moment felt lighter, lithe as when she was younger, eighteen, maybe nineteen. Nineteen was a better year. She was still blind then, so sure the world couldn't hurt her, and she could overcome anything it threw her way. Buoyancy, her grandmother had told her that young people have buoyancy.

Mika wandered along a cement-covered walkway leading to an open courtyard on the side of a building. Perhaps this was a memory, but the problem was that there was no one else around. That had never been the case at the University. Never when she'd been there had it been so deserted. She sank onto a bench, tucking her rebellious hair behind her ears. It was much shorter than she wore it in the present. Back then, it was just above her shoulders. She leaned back and breathed deeply in the air. Buoyancy, as Adele St. Clair called it, what a lovely feeling to revel in. It had been some time since she'd felt anything akin to this.

She didn't hear the footsteps or rustling that might have alerted her to his approach — entirely too caught up in the novelty of the moment. He was standing over her before she realized she wasn't alone anymore. It was startling, but then again, she wasn't afraid. Life at this isolated moment in her past had yet to teach her to be fearful. She stared into the face looking at her, a youngish face, a handsome face. He was not much older than her but familiar, clearly a visitor from a time yet to come.

"What are you doing?" she murmured.

"Do you like it here?" he asked flatly, glancing around.

"I did," she frowned. She sighed, thinking perhaps she liked it more when it felt like a forgotten memory. This man brought all sorts of messy complications in his wake.

He sat beside her on the stone bench, ostensibly invading her little buoyant haven, "Sorry, maybe I should have given you more time alone."

"Well, you could remedy that. You could leave," she grimaced in a perturbed affectation that she'd used as a younger woman but not for many years.

He chuckled, "I see. I guess it's better I didn't meet you twenty years ago. You probably would have shredded my dignity with no compunction."

She looked at the sky again, still lightly cloudy, with no sun in sight. "Maybe, if you deserved it."

And then she was silent. There were things to know that she didn't want to know. She'd rather cocoon herself in this feeling and pretend that the world was simple, as simple as one of those clouds drifting across the sky. He murmured, "We need to talk about a few things."

She laughed, "Why? I can't think of a good reason I'd want to talk right now."

"Yes, I can see that. Well, then, let's go for a walk. There's a coffee shop not far from here."

"You've been here before, James?" she asked, not knowing why she'd asked and immediately wishing she hadn't asked because the simple question intruded on this lovely reality.

He looked at her calmly, his eyes even in a young man's face with that steely bluish-gray color. "Yes, don't you remember Mika?" And at that remark, an odd feeling washed over her, then, in the next breath, dissipated and floated away. "How about that walk?" he asked casually, rising to his feet as though nothing unusual had been said. She stood up, suppressing the shiver that had traveled delicately through her, which was easily brushed aside as they began.

Every day for three days, he walked directly past the St. Clair mansion on Freret St. His expectations were amorphous, unformed. He kept an open mind, an open psyche, literally. It was the early seventies, and Gideon Reynolds was just a few months shy of thirty-five. The energies in the area were complicated, conflicted — some very powerful, others muddied, and then some perplexing. He'd come with the loose idea that he would see the Raybourne painting, perhaps obtain its return to a more protected cocoon. After all, just in passing, he could tell that the St. Clair women were an odd breed, unstable at best, all three of them, the mother, the daughter, and now the young granddaughter. Although, in passing, he had found her the most promising, very sensitive the young one.

She and her grandmother had gone for a walk in the area just yesterday, and Gideon had followed quite inconspicuously, trying to glean what he could.

He'd been up North in Maine just a week ago when the dreams had come — visions of this place, some red flood of danger, a danger that might crack everything open quite widely. Erratic as they might be, the energies in the St. Clair family line could be powerful, could be quite powerful in the wrong hands. And there was a definitive vulnerability, though where exactly it was seemed unclear.

Gideon wasn't what one might call a soft-spoken fellow, even in his thirties. Despite his philosophical hobbies, he could be described as a gruff man — tall, large-boned, and always carrying a few pounds beyond what one might consider suitable. He wore a thick beard and mustache, hair that was not fine but just crossing over onto the side of coarse, wavy, thick, and brown. His skin was more tanned, olive rather than fair. His mother had considered him a throwback to the distant Latin thread in the family. He'd always embraced his uniqueness. What some might consider a gruff nature, he turned to his advantage. But framed amidst his somewhat turbulent exterior were a set of pale blue eyes, eyes that absorbed nuances missed by most.

As he moved past the sprawling house that he loosely deemed a mansion, he noted something a bit different today, a new car in its spacious driveway. He meandered slowly, opening to another presence.

And then the doors of the front entrance swung open, and he shut down his psychic explorations. There was no need any longer. Very long strapping legs hosed in dark stockings sauntered down the front steps. He smiled. She wore a hat. That particular fashion trend was already in this decade, melting away. She leaned against the white sportscar and took out a cigarette.

White fitted skirt, black top, and face well shielded by her dipping hat — he paused near a tree across the street and allowed a brief glimpse into the interiors of what he thought was a very attractive woman. He liked people who knew who they were or at least pretended to.

And then he sighed deeply, the floods of red energy seeping painfully out of her. This one was all façade, a thin veneer covering a catastrophe. He watched Patrice Devalieur climb into her car as Gideon marked her energy so that she could be tracked later.

It was late afternoon, four o'clock to be exact — late enough for a glass of wine to commiserate her life in a small Italian restaurant on the corner of Royal Street. Patrice sipped her red wine and fingered the golden bracelet on her wrist, a gift from her boyfriend, although her mother had called it garish. In front of her daughter Mika, she had called it cheap and tasteless, something to suit her. She'd done this in front of her child, a child that seemed more her mother's than her own. Patrice quietly sipped her wine, numbing the volcanic surge of emotion within her. It was a temporary fix. This much she knew. But there were other numbing techniques to this brand of pain that had, in the last decade, become such a fixture in her soul.

"Patrice, when will you make a life for this poor child? If you're simply going to jump from man to man, then it would be better if you left her altogether. Leave her to me to raise." And she didn't even bother to have Dominique leave the room. The little girl stood beside her grandmother, pale and wide-eyed but expressionless. But then again, she must be used to these explosive emotional displays in front of her. Adele St. Clair wasn't one to shield her children from the ugly truths of life. She preferred for them to confront them head-on. And she, Patrice, in her mother's eyes, had reached that pinnacle of being one of the ugly truths of life.

Again, she sipped her wine. The small restaurant was practically deserted, and her waiter was skirting around the bar area, waiting for some signal from her that she wanted to order. She really should be getting ready to meet Adrien. There was a party tonight, late tonight. But as she sat in the dimly lit café, she felt all her will bleed out of her. The fact that she didn't care anymore seemed like a vast understatement. Not caring was bound to sum up more emotion than she felt capable of.

She sat there so deeply lost in that despairing black cave of her creation that she didn't notice the man entering the restaurant. She was oblivious to the exchange between him and the hostess. And she remained just as unaware until he was standing in front of her table. She glanced upward dismissively but was struck by an unexpected pair of pale blue eyes. She waited, unable to form any coherent response to this stranger's appearance at the side of her table.

There was a flicker of something in those eyes, something she couldn't pinpoint, although, regarding people, she had never cultivated any genuine perceptiveness. "I hope I'm not intruding."

His voice had nearly a graveled texture. And despite the compelling eyes, she didn't find him particularly handsome to her way of thinking. She shrugged, trying hard to salvage the veneer of indifference she had spent so many years perfecting. She took a small sip out of her glass. "Not especially. It's just me and my glass of wine," she murmured.

He nodded, "Ah, poor company for such a lovely lady."

She glanced up, explicitly frowning, "Well, Mr. Whoever you are, I should warn you that any charm is wasted on me today. Whatever you're selling, I'm not buying."

She clicked her long, manicured nails on the table, expecting him to evaporate beneath her excoriating reply. But he didn't leave, just stood there, looking at her calmly as though she were some naughty child having a tantrum. "Having a bad day, are we?" he replied nearly inaudibly.

She turned directly to him, feeling a well of fury bubble up in her from so many sources that she couldn't even begin to assess. "Having a bad life, and if you don't wish to become a casualty, I suggest you move along."

He laughed rather softly for such a gruff-looking man, "Perhaps, that is exactly what I wish."

"How delightful, another masochist, precisely what I need."

"You haven't a clue what you need. "

Her skin prickled up with irritation like a porcupine, "If you don't very much mind me asking, what the hell do you want?"

"I thought that was obvious, your delightful company."

"Are you out of your mind? Are you trying to pick me up here at four o'clock in the afternoon?"

He smiled, looking infuriatingly amused, "I see. A later hour might bring more success."

"The only thing that might bring you success today is a lobotomy on me."

He indicated the chair across from her, "How about I join you, and we can discuss it further?"

She rolled her eyes, completely unable to fathom what was happening here. "Have you escaped from a psycho ward? I thought I had made it clear. I am not interested in interacting with you or anyone for that matter."

Seemingly oblivious or possibly ignoring her, he slid into the chair across from her. "This is a nice place. I've been to the city several times but not here."

She was more than sure that her mouth was hanging open at his presumptuousness. She leaned back in the chair, feeling a novel flicker of fear travel up her spine. "You know, I can alert the management here and have you thrown out."

He nodded, pulling a cigarette case out of the inner pocket of his jacket and opening it. He glanced at her, those pale eyes disturbingly intense, "Do you smoke? I confess it's a habit I've yet to break. But then again, I find it hard to give up certain indulgences." He took out one cigarette and lit it, putting the case away, seemingly indifferent to her lack of response. After taking a puff from the cigarette and casually expelling it, he leaned back in his chair, continuing, "So, you were speaking of having me thrown out. Well, I suppose that is an option, but you might miss out on what promises to be a very intriguing conversation and possibly evening, Ms. Devalieur."

Her eyes widened, and her stomach sank as she heard her name roll off his lips. "How do you —" Then she stopped, feeling odd as though everything around her was crumbling.

"How do I know your name?" he finished her question. He signaled the waiter from across the room. "How about some more wine and possibly dinner? Would you like that, Patrice?"

Her name smoothly rolled off his tongue as though they were long acquaintances. She felt an odd combination of fear and languor taking her over. And then she felt his hand lightly cover hers. "No need to be frightened, my dear, not at all."

"Who are you?" she whispered shakily.

"A friend," he remarked decisively. As the waiter approached with menus, he murmured. "I need to know some things about you. And I want you to think before you answer me. What is happening in your life that is making you so sad?"

She looked at him with great confusion, feeling as though unless she could check it in a very few seconds, a great rain of tears was about to pour out of her.

An Old Wound

It was fairly late when he got in, just past midnight. He was staying at one of the larger hotels on Canal Street that remained active even at such an hour. Stopping at the bar, he got a drink — a scotch before heading up to his room.

When he entered, he slumped into the short green upholstered chair by the window and stared into the darkness of the New Orleans evening. The city felt turbulent to him, but then again, he had to admit that it could simply be touching the fringes of Patrice Devalieur's life that left him carrying the remnants of despair into this dark hour. He sipped his drink quietly, trying to distill all the varied impressions he'd gathered during their evening together.

Gideon wasn't an unfeeling man by any means, but he could disconnect. It was more than clear that what he could do for this woman was limited. Some kinds of damage ran deeper than others, and some actions could not be erased.

He sighed, oddly sad at this realization. He liked Patrice, and some choices she'd made were clearly driven by keen desperation. It was true that with dedication, she could remake her spirit and rebuild her life. But unfortunately, he erred not on the side of cynicism but instead realism. Old habits die hard, and a strong breeze would most likely blow her down a familiar path.

He closed his eyes and concentrated. The key here was damage control. She was being bled out, bled out of energy. The depression, the wild emotional tailspins, and erratic and reactive behavior could all be attributed to this. Like a doctor examining a sick patient, he had to diagnose the most chronic injuries first.

With great focus of attention, he created the image of Patrice in his mind and visualized her before him, sitting on the bed. Then he opened himself to this self-created image. He had spent enough time with her that evening, exploring her energies, her mind, to establish this connective collage that now appeared before him.

His gift was not centered in the visual arena but more so in the emotional one. Quietly, he asked, almost to himself, "Patrice, can you feel the source of the bleeding?"

"Bleeding?" the figure that took her shape echoed.

"Yes, can you feel its source?"

"Yes," calmly his mirage answered.

"Can you help me see?"

Again quietly, "Yes, perhaps, it's an old one."

He nodded slowly, "Of course, it would have to be."

It was fuzzy, oddly fuzzy. When she arrived at her small garden district home, there was a message from Adrien on her answering machine. His voice was icy and cutting. He was furious about her missing their engagement that evening without even calling. She stared up at the clock in her den. It was twelve-thirty. Her heart was beating quickly. She couldn't even remember why she hadn't called him. She was so tired, and her mind was so fuzzy.

Slowly, she sat down on her light blue tapestry sofa and tried to piece things together. She'd spent the evening with another man, a friend, she thought. But she couldn't remember his name and scarcely his face.

Her head was spinning. Maybe she'd been drinking too much. Maybe she should call Adrien. But all she felt was an aversion to that, strangely to him, at the moment.

She knew she should go and get ready for bed, but instead, she just laid back and fell into a deep, dreamless sleep.

Early in his indoctrination, Gideon had learned about the physical connection between the body and the spirit. As one of his greatest mentors had informed him, the body was merely a learning instrument of the spirit. But they were connected sometimes subtly and unexpectedly. The body could be affected in ways that touched the spirit, sometimes in profound ways that even damaged it. After all, reincarnation into the flesh was a dangerous proposition. Without question, it was the fastest place to learn and evolve but also an arena of significant vulnerability.

It wasn't difficult to track the man in question. He was still a photographer but not a very affluent one. His place of business was a souvenir shop in the French Quarter — not one of the better ones, one that had that intangible membrane of sleaziness about it.

As he entered the store, he noted a young girl behind the counter, perhaps early twenties. It crossed his mind that she had been ensnared in a similar situation, but he dismissed the thought. One consideration at a time, he told himself. Quite smoothly, he asked her if the owner was on the premises. And she smiled tentatively at him, a slight strain beneath her young eyes, making him wonder if, indeed, his suspicions were grounded.

The man appeared from the back room. He estimated that he was at least twenty years Patrice's senior. So, at that time, when she was sixteen, he would have been just a little older than Gideon was at present.

"Can I help you, sir?"

"Yes," he responded with an air of expectancy, the deliberate cadence of a man who was used to getting what he wanted. "I'm interested in securing specific items that I understand you are able to deliver."

The man seemed a little shaken by his directness. He was slight and wiry, as though already his body was succumbing to age. "Yes, well, what kind of items? I am, after all, a reputable businessman."

Gideon narrowed his eyes. It took great control not to flatten this reprehensible excuse for a man right where he stood. But really, who was he to judge? He pressed on, "I'm interested in pictures. Is that clear enough for you?"

The man's eyes widened and then took on a predatory gleam. "Of course, maybe you could step into my office."

Gideon nodded and followed him into one of the shadowy corners of the small souvenir shop.

"Hello," Patrice answered the phone on the nightstand in her bedroom. She glanced at the clock beside it. It was nearly one. She'd spent most of the day in bed once she'd awoken on the sofa. Oddly, she'd slept the whole night there, still dressed from the day before.

She'd expected Adrien to call at some point, but he hadn't. She was sure his injured pride prevented it, but she hadn't felt inclined to try to make excuses.

"Patrice."

"Yes." the voice startled her but brought back a flood of disconnected memories from the night before. Had he held her? Had he kissed her goodnight passionately, or was that an odd, unmeshed dream? So much of it was unclear, so much.

"For a moment, I wasn't sure you were there. How are you today, my dear?"

Her heart was hammering oddly. She felt so confused, so perplexed by it all. "I don't know. I'm a little foggy about things, about last night."

"Yes, to be expected. Why don't you rest, and I'll pick you up later for dinner?"

"Dinner?" She asked, still feeling confused by it all.

"Yes, about six. I have a few things to take care of." She swallowed, wondering what she should do. "It's all right," he said, then hung up.

He stared at the brown envelopes of photos and negatives on the desk before him. Hopefully, by this evening, the matter would be cleared up. He rubbed his head. It was throbbing acutely. He'd left Samuel Armstrong with quite an impression, an impression he wasn't likely to shake for some time.

The office had been small, cramped, and smelling quite musty as though there was water seepage somewhere. And there was another door beyond it that was closed, a darkroom Gideon suspected. Business of this kind was likely not to be left in the hands of others.

Armstrong seemed shocked when he voiced the name. He actually looked quite squeamish. "St. Clair? What makes you think I'd have pictures of a St. Clair? That's an old family in this city."

Gideon had smiled and pressed on, "I've been told. Others have undoubtedly paid for them."

"Not many. You have to be careful. Enemies of a sort can be dangerous around here."

"So, they do exist?" he asked.

Armstrong smiled smugly, "For a price, they exist."

Quite coolly, he inquired. "How did you ever manage to get them, a St. Clair girl?"

The man before him laughed, "A long time ago, unhappy young girls come rich and poor. But they all operate the same, so needy, so easy to control."

Gideon felt the coldness of resolve wrap around him at these words. "Let's see them first. Then we'll talk price."

Without much hesitation, the shopkeeper opened a nearby file cabinet and flipped through a multitude of folders before he reached what he was looking for. He abruptly plopped it down on the table directly in front of Gideon. "These are my last copies, but I can make more. I have the negatives."

Gideon didn't move to open the envelope, just very calmly stared at the man before him. "Now, I'll have the negatives too, and the names of everyone who has a copy of these."

The small man before him just stared blankly for a moment, then laughed as the impact of the words hit him. "What are you talking about?"

Gideon flexed his hand, focusing great energy into it until its temperature began to climb. "I'd advise you to do this, Mr. Armstrong, and possibly rethink your life choices in the process." He carefully placed one hand over Samuel Armstrong's mouth while the other began to scorch into his flesh.

As the evening approached, Gideon had retrieved three of the photo packets. Tomorrow, he would obtain the fourth, and this particular problem would be solved. Clearly, it was not Patrice's only problem, but it would stop a specific sort of vulnerability that was eroding her natural defenses. He checked his watch. It was nearly five. In just an hour, he would see her and then decide how to proceed.

The envelopes lay in a stack on the small round table before him. The three gentlemen in question proved to be less tenacious than Armstrong. Then again, they were voyeurs. They hadn't spent a lifetime as a pornographer exploiting children.

He picked up one envelope, somewhat indecisive about opening it, but then again, it was necessary. He pulled out the first picture of Patrice, Patrice as a young girl. It was a nude lying on a dingy sofa somewhere — no doubt in Armstrong's apartment. Her eyes were glazed, alcohol perhaps, but something else beyond that. Yes, of course, a tool of the trade, he'd probably slipped drugs into her drink. Just for a moment, he let himself feel the fear, the confusion. *"So beautiful, Patrice. We must capture your beauty."* He could hear his coaxing of her. He'd lavished her with attention, the attention she seemed oddly starved for.

And then he concentrated elsewhere. Armstrong had pulled energy from Patrice through the photo, but this also had been done recently. The second man he'd sold them to as a novelty two years ago. He was a drainer. He'd pulled so much from her that it caused a profound emotional unbalance in her, at times suicidal. For a moment, he used the picture to send her his own energy directly through her exposed heart area, further cementing the energy he'd given her the night before. He could feel more calmness and a bit more serenity around her now.

Quickly, he flipped through the other two photos, more of the same. And then checked the negatives. All was there. He was sure of it. Armstrong was frightened out of his mind when he'd left him. He was quite sure he thought he was encountering some sort of demon. Gideon laughed to himself. He supposed he'd been called worse.

In the hour before he went to Patrice, he tore all the photos into pieces and burned them and the negatives on top of a plate he'd eaten his lunch on.

True Sight

The week, or was it weeks they spent together, felt altogether separate from reality. She moved through the day and nights as though she were another person, perhaps from a book somewhere, wholly disconnected from what had been.

They spent the days traveling through the city or in the country outside of it and spent the nights together in a small house that he had rented near Audubon Park, where they would often take long walks. She'd told a few people, her mother who was keeping Mika, and some friends, that she was going on a holiday. She hadn't told Adrien anything. He'd left a few messages on her answering machine, then stopped, but, of course, she hadn't returned to her house in days. It was late February, so some nights were chilled in the small, sparsely furnished house. They would often light the fireplace and just sit in front of it. They talked but not of things that altered this strange bubble she found herself in.

One night she did ask him pointedly, "Are you married?"

He glanced back toward her with a curious smile. He held a brandy in his hands and had been staring out a window across the semi-darkened room. She was sitting on a small rug in front of the fireplace. It had been silence between them. That wasn't unusual. Quite often, they would lapse into long, uninterrupted silences. "Do you think I am?" Gideon answered calmly.

She stared at him for a moment somewhat intensely, then answered, "No, I think that would be too simple."

He laughed briefly, sort of a low rumble she had become accustomed to in their days together. Clearly, she amused him. In fact, often, it seemed. "And you don't think it's that simple."

She shook her head, "No, and I don't think you love me. I've known men who loved me, and you don't act as they did at all."

He moved closer, settling in a chair near her. "You shouldn't worry about such things."

She sat up on her knees, looking at him with sadness. "I can't help but yearn for some permanency. It's my nature."

He nodded slowly, "Would you come away with me and change your life completely?"

She hesitated, "Are you asking me too?"

"Would you consider it?" She looked away toward the flames, wondering if she would.

It had caught her off-guard, a bit like a gut punch. Their time together had such an unreal quality, but was it possible for this to be real life? "I'd consider it. I feel peaceful with you."

He lightly touched her hair and gently tilted her chin toward him before kissing her.

When Patrice recalled their time together, it would be with no substance. It was more like a lovely dream that she had awoken from. She did consider his offer, but such a change to her seemed like an unreachable ascent upon a frightening mountain.

"Why are we here?"

"There are some things I'd like you to see."

It was difficult to focus. Moments before, they'd been sipping coffee on a lovely little patio of a pastry shop not far from Loyola University. They'd walked there, maybe, but she didn't remember walking. Quite suddenly, events had folded in upon themselves, and then they were settled, enjoying a warm afternoon breeze.

But again, now, everything had shifted.

"James," she murmured, and within the span of thought, he was standing beside her, not young as he'd been at Loyola but older as when she first met him. Was it a day ago? It felt longer, much longer. "What's happening? I feel dizzy."

"It's all right," he moved closer to her, taking her hand in his, then things began to calm.

She knew where she was now. They were back at the mall, the downtown mall in Charlottesville. Where he had—

"Focus on this moment. What do you see?" His measured voice cut firmly through her recollections.

"People." she glanced around. It was different, daytime, and busier, much busier than it had been the night before.

"Yes."

"Just people, nothing special."

He squeezed her hand, and she knew there was something she should remember. "Now, look closer, Mika."

She began to feel the dizziness again and a sound in her ears, building like a soft hum. Her vision blurred over a bit. "I don't know what—" abruptly, she stopped because something was happening. The image of the people blurred, and then after, she could only see their outlines, forms becoming inconsistent, fluctuating, and suddenly great outreaches of color around them, from them, permeating throughout, pulsating. "What is this?"

"True sight Dominque," her name lightly flowed from his lips.

It was all so disorienting, but as vision she was accustomed to returned a bit, she could focus on an elderly couple not far from them, holding hands. And then, her sight shifted again, and she could see great splashes of blue, white, and green color being shared between them, fluctuating back and forth, intertwining. "Soulmates," he whispered beside her. "They share much more than their lives. They share their energy. They truly operate as one." It was dazzling to see. She felt warmth around her heart, just watching them.

And then, in the very next moment, she began to feel an odd irritation on her neck, causing her to turn around. Across the pavement, standing in front of a shop window, was another couple, a younger couple who appeared to be no older than their middle twenties. She swallowed as a trickle of anxiety permeated her former sense of well-being. "What are you feeling?" James coaxed.

"Something's wrong," she whispered. The unease grew the more she focused on them. Then, out of nowhere, there was a sharp stab around her heart area and shortness of breath. "It's difficult to breathe."

"Be careful. It appears you're very empathic, tapping into emotions." So disturbing, she couldn't see the lovely cascade of colors flowing from these two as it had in some of the others.

"I can't see their energy."

"Energy occurs in frequencies. The positive auras you saw before operated with a higher vibration. To see the others, you must focus down to a lower level."

"Lower?" But even as she said it, she could feel it. Her vision began to adjust, and it felt as though even the air around her had a thicker, heavier quality. It reminded her of the days in New Orleans during the summer when the humidity was so thick that you could feel it like a film on your skin. But this was so much more, ten times that, and so horribly dense. "James, I can't do this."

"I know it's difficult, but it's important. Try to see."

Again, she forced herself to focus on the younger couple. The young man took the girl's hand, but it differed from the other two. It felt oddly aggressive, and the woman just seemed to allow it as though—

"She had to —" James completed her thought.

"Where is their energy? I still can't see anything."

"It's complicated. Relationships are so much more important than people ever acknowledge, so beneficial at times, and at others—"

"At others?" she repeated, asking, but not wanting to go further because she knew, somewhere she already knew.

Then she began to see. It started slowly, as an ugly yellow color almost imprinted on parts of the girl, her arms, and her chest, as though his hands had marked her. And then there was more, a strange heavy fog around them, a mist, ugly and gray. "I see a gray fog. Is that their energy, this muddy gray?"

"Not exactly, more of camouflage, I'd say. This one is complete."

"Complete? What does that mean?"

"This drainer, the man, some who take energy are fractured, flawed, and easier to spot, but some are quite adept at it."

She returned her gaze to them. The fog around them was so dense, so heavy. "Are you saying he's taking her energy?"

"Of course, Mika, it's quite common. There are parasites among every species, and we've all been drainers in some incarnation. It's a level of learning. We have to learn to evolve without, well, doing this."

She looked back and focused in more deliberately, wholly determined to see. "Be careful. You should prepare yourself," he murmured. But she was fixed, so fixed that she felt her body tremble in the effort, and her vision began to flicker. But with the sheer force of will, she pierced the gray mist around them. And she wished, she wished as she often had in her lifetime that she had left well enough alone.

There were colors from the girl — pink, orange, and even red, painful colors of emotion and energy that felt like confusion. She could see them forcibly being ripped from her and drawn into him. But she didn't just see it. Somehow, she felt the sickening feeling, the frigid coldness. Her breath labored as he took and took and took.

"Why is this happening?" she whispered.

"Relationships are precarious things. Much can be gained from some but so much lost as well from others."

It was questionable to say when he first noticed that there was a tangible nature to the darkness. At least in some places, it was palpable, expressive, and constricting. Tonight, he felt it more pronounced than at other times, as though something was hunting, predatory, surrounding the house. He sat quietly, staring out into the night. It was impossible to see down to the water or make out anything but malformed shadows bending and mutating in the darkness.

He bent his head, closing his eyes. He felt movement, whispering movement. Opening them slowly, he waited, watching the closed door leading to his bedroom. It was sometime after two in the morning. Almost silently, the door swung open. She stood there in the frame, staring back at him. He tried to read her mood, and then he smiled. It was blocked, shut off. She was protecting herself. Surprising, maybe not, so much was stirring in her that was formerly untapped. Still, there was little movement, although she did run her hand through the mass of dark hair. "Are you going to join me?"

Wide, dark eyes in a very pale face, reminding him of a painting, oddly enough, reminding him of the painting in question, "I'm trying to decide if I should start screaming or just look for a weapon," she said rather stoically.

"Well, screaming is a little useless out here, and I can assure you, Mika, that you don't need a weapon."

The response was quiet but determined, "I am not reassured. What kind of game are you playing?"

"No game. I couldn't let you leave, not yet."

She glanced around a bit furtively. She was contemplating an escape route. He couldn't blame her there, after what had occurred earlier. Although, at present, he wasn't at all sure what she remembered of their recent astral journey after her collapse. And then she took a step away from the bedroom door, though not precisely in his direction, not exactly progress. "What is it that you want, James?"

He stood up, and that sudden movement caused her to back away just a bit. "To be frank, Mika Devalieur, I'm not exactly sure, but I know you are a key."

The fear kicked in, and he felt her in motion toward the front hallway before she began her trek. The long dark hair wisped around her shoulders as she moved like lightning. He reached her seconds after her hand closed on the doorknob. His hands grasped her cool pale arms, and he crushed down upon blue velvet. *You aren't leaving yet? We've hardly even begun.*

Her dark eyes were brimming with fear of the unknown. "This is far beyond me, Sir. What you are doing here is unnatural."

He breathed in the cold air and the heavy smell of paint fumes in the studio. And his head spun as did his senses.

James felt the room bend and shift, as did her willowy form in his hands. Again, he stared into her eyes, the same eyes but different, the same expression brimming with shock and fear. His hands bit down into her arms, too tightly, he thought somewhat distantly, but he couldn't be sure. "What did you say?" he whispered.

"You're hurting me," was the quiet but steely reply. And then he released her, letting his hands drop completely to his sides. It was foolish. She would probably run, and he would never see her again, or perhaps he would soon be in the company of many armed policemen coming to arrest him for kidnapping. But he was far too drained and overcome to do anything else. He stood there at the doorway of his home waiting, for something, for anything.

But Mika's wide dark eyes gave away nothing. They were shadowed. Silently, they moved past his face, scanning the insides of his house as though they were looking for something, looking to glean something. And then they focused on his face again with a surprising look of curiosity, expectancy. Surely a reaction he had not calculated. "Why didn't you tell me, James?"

He leaned back against the doorframe, feeling acutely as though nothing at all would support the languidness that had taken occupation of him, nothing at all. "Tell you?" he asked.

She nodded, "Yes, it took me a while to put it together. But you're him. You're the shadow creature."

A chill passed over him, and he closed his eyes, letting his chin sink onto his chest in pure exhaustion. How he wished that statement was as nonsensical as it sounded to his ears.

A Shadow

Her grandmother's house was not always welcoming. It was often cold and drafty in unusual, unexpected places. There was a particular spot in the bedroom where she stayed that always seemed chilled. It wasn't near a window, near a door, or near a vent. Her Gran had a rug placed over the wooden floor, but the cold draft seemed higher. In the winter, she had a small space heater placed along the wall, but as Mika passed by, she noted nothing had changed. The chill remained. Adele had the attic above the room checked, but there were no openings or damages to the insulation. She suggested Mika pick another room. After all, the small mansion was filled with them, but she was reluctant. The familiarity of the space was a comfort to her. Good and bad, she knew it well. It was consistent, even with its cold spot. It was a touchstone in a life where inconsistency was the norm. She stopped talking about the cold spot. Although it didn't change, it also never interfered with her.

When she was around twelve, she first saw the shadow move across the room. It was fall. She remembered this because she'd left the window open to allow the cool air inside. Her sheer, rose-colored drapes moved ever so slightly that evening in the night breeze. Her eyes took in the clock on her bedside table, three fifteen. She had no idea why she'd awoken, just that she had, and then she relaxed, intending to return to sleep. When she first saw it, her eyes had glazed over a bit, slightly out of focus, but there it was, a clear shadow moving deliberately across her room. She sat up, rubbing her eyes, then refocusing. But it had disappeared. She decided then that she must tell her grandmother to have her eyes checked. She might need glasses.

But, by morning, it was forgotten, and she didn't even think about it for weeks until it happened again.

"You must strip away from your mind things that are imaginings."

"Imaginings?"

"Fears, worries, what you project will be, all of this disturbs your peace of mind and is useless to you."

James flopped back dramatically onto his aunt's oriental rug, where he'd been sitting for what felt like an eternity. But it took only an arch of his aunt's eyebrow to make him sit up again and assume the familiar cross-legged stance. Aubrey Mayhew, sister to his Uncle Gideon, was attempting to teach a very independent-minded and, at times, rebellious fifteen-year-old boy the fine art of meditation. Though he complied, he frowned in mild disdain, "So, you're saying my thoughts are useless."

She almost smiled but not quite. His aunt was still a young woman, just into her forties, with a fine-boned face and a lush head of dark blond hair. And, of course, blue eyes. Uncle Gideon said they were Scottish eyes that masked a quick temper. The temper he rarely saw, just mainly the measured, steely determination.

"Meditation has little to do with thought. It is about feeling. So many thoughts lead us on a train of projection that never comes to pass, only guiding us into a place of exhaustion or frustration, such a waste of time and energy."

He conceded, somewhat reluctantly, "Yes, I suppose I can see that."

She nodded authoritatively, "James, you must learn to gain mastery over your mind. It will open new worlds for you if you can clear it and control the extraneous."

He straightened his back and closed his eyes, again trying to clear his cluttered mind. He was being trained. It had begun with real vigor last summer after his birthday. Before that, the family had seemed content to allow him to dabble as he wished in the extracurricular activities of his lineage. But once he was fifteen, something had changed, and all had proceeded at a grueling pace.

"Have you cleared your mind?"

"Yes, Aunt Aubrey, it's as vacant as my geometry homework."

"James, if you don't take this seriously —"

"No worries, I'm serious, Auntie." She hated when he called her Auntie. And yes, he was bucking the pressure inflicted upon him. Why precisely he needed to meditate when he could be doing so many other things was, in his opinion, unfair.

"Now," was all she instructed. And his experience of her was the more abbreviated her speech, the fewer antics she was willing to indulge.

With a deep breath, he settled in, allowing the cumbersome thoughts of the day to float away.

And surprisingly enough, this time, it didn't take long before he began to feel pulled, pulled to another place, another room in someone else's house where a young girl was asleep in a bed.

Mika's eyes marked the shadow as it crossed the room, then hesitated near the window. She didn't move, didn't dare, for that certainly would cause it to disappear if it was real at all.

Of course, the first thing that crossed her mind was the story of Peter Pan. Her Gran had read it to her when she was very young, but this wasn't like that. This wasn't without peril. It chilled her to think this way, but for some reason, it felt like she was potentially in great jeopardy. She closed her eyes, concentrating, and instead of speaking, sent out a thought to the room.

"Are you dangerous?"

She opened her eyes and noticed the shadow was still on the far wall facing her. Again, she closed her eyes, wondering why she was continuing this way, *"Are you real?"*

She waited this time and listened quietly, internally, and finally, an answer came to her in a murmur, *"Yes, real."*

She opened her eyes again, but the shadow had vanished completely.

James felt himself return to his body in something of a yank. Opening his eyes, he stared into the displeased face of his aunt. "Where were you?" she asked a bit sternly.

"I-I don't know," he sort of choked out because his head was spinning outrageously. "Somewhere else."

She walked over to him abruptly, kneeling unceremoniously down next to him, then grabbing his arm and closing her eyes.

"Aunt—"

"Quiet," she snapped, cutting him off.

After a moment, she focused on him, staring intently. "Well, I didn't expect this so quickly, but it seems you have an aptitude for traveling, James."

"Traveling, what does that mean?"

"Astral projection usually takes years to master, but you're quick, aren't you?" she commented, straightening up.

A little shakily, he got to his feet, feeling some definitive aches from the prolonged awkward positioning. "So, you're saying I traveled out of my body."

"Yes, James, but you should be careful."

"Careful? I thought you wanted me to do this."

"Yes, but about going there. It isn't time for that yet."

"There was a young girl there."

"Yes, and you'll see her again one day but not for a while. Everything in its time."

He looked into her wide eyes, staring at him, not with fear, but something else. Perhaps he was being self-indulgent, but it felt keenly now that pieces were beginning to fit together.

"The shadow creature," he repeated slowly.

She flinched a bit when he said it aloud, "I suppose that sounds crazy."

He smiled, "Crazy? No, I just didn't know that was what you called it," he shrugged a bit, "or me. It sounds so nefarious."

"I was twelve."

"Yeah, and it looked like—"

"A shadow traveling across my room that I was able to speak to."

He looked around with a bit of disorientation, realizing that they were still standing poised by his front door, which, moments before, Mika had been intent on fleeing through. "Do you want to go sit down and talk about this?"

She flung her long dark hair behind her shoulders in exasperation. "I don't know, James. All of this, it is crazy, but—"

"But," he repeated softly because it had to be her. It had to be her decision to walk through the door, the metaphorical door, hopefully not actually out of his front door.

"I-I can't understand what's happening. But it feels like—"

He reached out and grasped her arm. This wasn't fair. He'd had a lifetime of preparation, but Mika's life was changing profoundly over the course of a few days. "Let's go sit. I promise I'll be harmless."

She nodded slowly, "First, answer me. The shadow creature, I'm not losing my mind. You were connected to it."

"Yes," he said quietly, "I was."

He wasn't supposed to return, but he did. Mostly when she was asleep, he would see the room. Vision in the astral form was nothing like it was with physical eyes. Sometimes he would travel that great house, noting all the things that physical eyes couldn't see —the trapped spirits, ghosts, if you will, visiting spirits, and energy imprints throughout. It was a difficult place, so layered with problematic pockets of thick energy. Even in the girl's room, where she stayed, because he noted that she didn't stay there all the time, there was a disturbing energy imprint. A suicide of a servant there a century before had left a heavy collection of dense, negative energy marking the event. But strangely, the girl seemed able to circumvent it, as though she were somehow protected and would naturally avoid that particular spot.

And then, there was the other matter. On the second floor was a locked room that he could not enter. Even in his astral state, he could not enter, though what he could sense was powerful energy, energy that he was not allowed to approach for some reason.

Then one afternoon, it had all ended.

"James, your aunt tells me you've continued to visit the house in the south." His uncle had come into town and asked to go for a walk with him. Uncle Gideon had been unusually quiet until they reached a wooden bench in a park a few blocks from his house, where they settled, watching some children play on a swing set not far from them.

He straightened up, suddenly becoming nervous at the stern tone. "Yes, I have."

He nodded, looking off in the distance as though focusing on something far away. "You know, our family has a very specific lineage. We're not just here to live out our lives as everyone else does. We're here to help humanity evolve and protect them when necessary."

"Protect them, from what exactly?"

"Some call it evil. We call it the low ones, the ones who seek chaos, discord, and power over others. Our particular bloodline has always followed this path wherever it leads, and you are no exception."

"What does that have to do with that house, with the—"

"Girl?" his uncle finished for him. "Tell me. Why did you continue to travel there?"

He shook his head, wondering why, indeed. "Honestly, I don't know. I felt drawn. There's something about her, something so familiar."

"Kindred," his uncle commented. "I understand. I can tell you that as your aunt indicated, you will meet her again. But for now, you both have your own lives to lead. We are almost certain she has a part to play in all of this."

"But she's not part of our bloodline," he said. But his uncle didn't answer, just forbid him to return there, which he didn't, not ever again.

They settled in the den, and he noted from a rustic wall clock near the fireplace that it was just nearing three in the morning. His mother had always told him that three o'clock was a very active spiritual time. Mika sat on the edge of the sofa, and he in a chair near her. It crossed his mind how beautiful she was. Even in her anxious, tousled, fearful state, something about her drew him fiercely. Somewhere in the roar of everything else that was happening, that had become lost. That elemental attraction remained, a draw he felt to her from the moment they first spoke, perhaps even before when he'd returned to a house he'd later been forbidden to.

"What do you want to know?" he said.

She looked at him wide-eyed. Of course, he could see it, complete overload, a feeling he was familiar with. "Why am I here? It's clear now this goes way beyond the Raybourne."

He nodded slowly, "Yes, it begins with the Raybourne but goes far, far beyond. Your grandmother, Adele St. Clair, did she ever speak of Devon Carlyle?"

"Devon Carlyle? The man who gave her the painting? No, never, I never heard his name until you spoke it."

"Well, as I said, he was my Great Uncle, and he did give your grandmother the Raybourne. But what you don't know Mika," he paused, wondering what would happen next, what would happen in this very next moment, and how they would come to live again once it had passed. "What you don't know, Mika is that Devon Carlyle was also your grandfather."

Her eyes widened. "What-what are you saying?"

"I'm saying that your mother was the child of Devon Carlyle and Adele St. Clair."

Unforeseen

It wasn't fair, not any of it. She held the newborn child against her chest and, instead of warmth, felt a coldness creeping into her heart. And then, she handed the infant to her mother, who was looking at her with genuine concern.

"I'm just tired," she murmured. Adele had spent the whole day in labor with her mother at her side as George was still stationed overseas. And she'd thought, hoped that everything would be healed and new again once she held the child in her arms. But nothing, nothing had turned out as she'd expected.

"I told you that this was not going to happen," she'd whispered.

He nodded but continued to walk next to her, seemingly undaunted by her declaration.

"Are you listening to me?" she asked, a curious sort of panic rising inside her.

Again, he nodded but said nothing. And then she stopped and pulled her hand from his. He turned to look at her, virtually expressionless.

"I want to go home," she said.

"I know you do, and I'm sorry."

"Sorry for what?" she asked, overcome with anxiety and a tinge of inexplicable dread.

"Sorry that you're unhappy and can't accept what will be. You can't change it any more than I."

She just stood there, staring at him, completely swept up in desolation — feeling as though if she let it, all of it would swallow her whole.

After all, she hadn't intended for things to go as they had. It simply wasn't fair.

It was their fourth meeting. Every Tuesday, then Thursdays, they'd meet at the park, walk, and talk about things, all sorts of things. She told herself that it was a friendship, a peculiar, harmless friendship, except, of course, that first kiss. But nothing since then. He was someone to simply confide in until George came home again. And once he did, things would resume as they had before, and George would take his place. But the truth was that George had never really been her friend. He didn't listen to her, laugh with her, or seem to have an intrinsic understanding of her like this man.

"Devon, I am a married woman." Was she saying this for him or herself?

He frowned, grasping the hand she'd so unceremoniously taken away from him only seconds before. "Yes, Adele, of that I am very much aware." He pulled her closer, lightly kissing her on the cheek, and she felt a blush and trembling rise up in her from everywhere. Is this what passion felt like? Was this what it was to fall in love?

Of course, she was lying to herself from the beginning. From those first flirtatious moments they'd spent together, she knew. This was no friendship. It was an attraction, a forbidden attraction that she felt powerless to resist. Although she tried to stop, she couldn't. She continued to see him but always fought it at the same time.

"What exactly do you expect me to do? Have an affair with you, then go back to my husband?"

"Of course, not Adele. You can come with me. Come with me back to Scotland."

There was emotion, so much emotion. In fact, at times, she felt bottlenecked with emotion, as though with the slightest push, it would erupt uncontrollably out of her. "How could I? A divorce? My family would disown me. How could I?"

Sometimes he would look at her with pity. She hated that as though she was babbling nonsense. How could it be so simple for him? Then again, he was a man, unconnected, free in the world to do as he pleased. It wasn't fair that she should feel this. Why couldn't she just feel this way about George? Why couldn't life be simple?

"We're not here for a simple life. That's not what life is about."

"What did you say?"

There were times, she remembered, that Devon would do this. It was as though he'd heard her thoughts aloud, then responded to them.

He'd rented rooms in a house off Walnut Street. On their fifth meeting, he took her there, discretely entering the house from a back entrance up a short flight of stairs. She remembered the smell of cinnamon in the first sitting room as he then took her inside to the bedroom.

"Devon," she'd whispered, not at all sure what she wanted to say, but by then, he'd started kissing her softly and making her forget why all of this was wrong. That day, they'd spent the afternoon together in bed, making love, and he'd promised her many things. And just before they left, he showed her the Raybourne for the first time.

"What did you say?"

"I know this is hard to soak in, but Devon Carlyle is your grandfather. He and your grandmother had an affair, and your mother was their child."

James could see and, more than that, feel how Mika was struggling with this revelation. Her face had paled since he first told her, and her eyes had widened under the stress. "That doesn't sound at all like my grandmother."

"You know, it makes things easier if you can let go of preconceived ideas and judgments of people. Before she was your grandmother, she was a young woman with a life, with her own hopes, dreams, and maybe disappointments."

"How-how could you possibly know this?"

He took a moment, trying to frame the answer appropriately. Of course, he shouldn't be surprised how quickly she would get to the heart of the matter. "My family, my family line is somewhat unique, Mika. We have gifts and abilities, and there are significant markers in our bloodline."

"Markers?" she hesitated, "What are you talking about, DNA?"

"No, not exactly. If you take a moment and think back, clear your mind a bit, you might begin to recall things that happened recently that might seem extraordinary."

She looked at him blankly for a moment, and he wondered if indeed she could remember, if she could remember the astral traveling or if it had been relegated to the realm of dreams or fantasies as people most often did who experienced such things. "I'm not sure exactly what—" then her voice faded off, and he'd felt a sharp intake of breath in her, although it was inaudible.

"Do you remember the old couple on the downtown mall and then seeing them as they actually were?"

She didn't answer, just continued to stare at him in a bit of shock.

"Can you remember the other couple, the younger one?"

The silence seemed to go on forever, and finally, the softest answer was "Yes" in a mere whisper. "You said he was draining her."

He reached out and took her hand in his. It was cool, nearly icy to his touch. Was it fear? But he didn't feel fear. Something else, she was moving within, evolving, taking her first steps into a new realm, and it was amazing and catastrophic in the same instant. Because he remembered when it had happened to him, but he'd had so much more time to prepare. "He was."

"It was terrible," she murmured.

"It is part of life."

She was breathing deeply, and he squeezed her hand. "You said there were markers."

"Yes, by seeing, really seeing as you and I did not long ago, it became known that your mother was part of our lineage, bloodline if you will, as are you."

"You're saying we're related."

"Yes, cousins, third or fourth, I'm not really sure."

"But my mother never showed any special, I mean, is it abilities? I don't know what to call this."

He smiled, "Abilities will do for now. There is always free will, Mika. As you choose whether or not to develop latent talents in any direction, you must choose this as well."

"And this, this explains the oddness of your behavior. I don't mean that as it sounds, but I don't know why I'm here right now. What's happened. What you did to me."

"I gave you energy, powerful, directed energy so that you could tap into some of your abilities."

She nodded slowly, then pulled her hand from his, and clasped them in her lap. He knew she was trying to soak in what he'd told her. It was a lot. He could feel it as nearly a panic rising in her. What she needed now more than anything was energy, and given their unique connection, he knew exactly how to give her some, though how she'd react was another matter.

"Mika," her eyes met his, clouded, confused. "It's all right."

"I don't know. All of this seems a bit crazy."

"Yes, I can see why you'd think so."

"And beyond that, what in the world does all of this have to do with that painting?"

He stared at her, saying nothing for a moment. "I would have thought that you had guessed by now."

"Guessed? Guessed what that—" then she stopped abruptly as she made the connection. "Raybourne, the artist, he was—" again, she halted because in voicing it, one more door would swing open and so many others already had this evening.

"Yes, yes, one of us as well."

It was more than impossible to explain what she saw and what she felt when she stared at the painting. "Who did you say the artist was?"

"Henry Joseph Raybourne, he painted it in 1902."

It was propped up against the wall, situated on a small night table near the brass double bed where she and Devon had just spent several hours together. It looked so oddly out of place in this sparsely decorated room with its elegant, burnished gold frame and rich, vibrant colors. "It looks like it belongs in a museum," Adele murmured but knowing at the same time that she didn't believe that. It shouldn't be in a cold, stark setting like a museum but in someone's home, protected. And then she sat up, pulling the bedsheets more tightly around her. Such strange thoughts. "What are you going to do with it?"

He sat down with a bounce on the bed next to her. He'd been dressing while she hadn't noticed. He smiled in that engaging way of his, the engaging way that had seduced a married woman into bed with him not so many hours ago. But then she sighed deeply because it was a lie. She'd come to this place willingly, not because he wanted her to but because something inside her needed to. She'd never be able to explain this to anyone except him, Devon, the man in the center of this hurricane with her. "The painting? I don't know. You though, I'd thought I'd buy dinner somewhere for my lovely lady."

She smiled sadly, "I don't know, Devon. We might be seen."

"Would you come with me back to Scotland, Adele?"

"I-I don't know, Devon. I have a life here."

"A husband you don't love and a life you're stagnating in."

"How do you know that I don't love him?"

He took her hand, slowly kissing it, then grasping it firmly. "Because you love me, that's more than clear, my darling."

She frowned, looking down at their two hands intertwined. He was right. She didn't want him to be right, but he was. As the tears threatened to overflow from her eyes, she answered, "I need some time."

"I have to leave at the end of the week, but I'll be back. And then we can make plans." Slowly, he tipped her chin upwards. "All right?"

She nodded, "Yes, yes, all right." Softly he kissed her on the lips, the slightest brush of a kiss that made her believe, believe that it was possible.

"All right," he repeated softly. "And Adele, I'll need a favor. I need you to keep the painting until I return."

She glanced back at it across the small room. And just a whisper floated through her mind. *Keep her safe.*

"Yes, I will until you get back." And then he smiled at her, making her believe that it was possible, that happiness was within her reach.

Four weeks later, she received a telegram from a man identifying himself as a friend of Devon Carlyle, telling her that Devon had been killed in a car accident in Scotland. He asked her to keep the painting in her safekeeping.

The last time Adele had seen him alive, he told her only to give the painting to him or someone who said these curious words to her — *As Above, So Below.*

She'd laughed, thinking them nonsensical. But she never saw Devon again, except in dreams when he would hold her and promise they would be together one day.

And two months after he'd gone, she realized she was pregnant.

The Path

His words resounded in her mind. *He was one of us.* But it was too much in the moment, too much to absorb the implications of anything. She stood up silently and walked across the room, saying nothing, not knowing what to say. Was this true? Was any of what James was telling her even remotely possible?

"I know it's a lot," he said quietly from across the room.

She didn't answer. Her mind was too busy whirling. First, her Gran, she remembered her from when she was young with her mother Patrice, always cold, distant, fighting, disapproving. In fact, she could barely scrape up a civil memory in their history. "It doesn't make sense," she murmured, almost to herself. Always, always, her grandmother had implied her mother's shortcomings were at fault. By the time she was ten, it had been repeatedly and effectively drilled into her head what a terrible mother Patrice had been and how she had failed her young daughter.

"You might need to give this a rest Mika. You're so tired."

She turned around slowly, facing James, who hadn't moved from the armchair he'd been sitting in at the beginning of their conversation. "What did you say?" she whispered.

James wasn't even looking at her, just leaning forward and staring, his hands clasped in his lap. "Puzzling things out, it might be best to let it lie. You're exhausted. Your energy is very low."

"How did you know I—"

"The truth or what's convenient to believe?" he cut her off softly.

Then he stood up but made no move to come closer to her. "What does that mean?" she demanded, needing, not even really understanding what exactly she was needing.

"You're upset after everything we've discussed and trying to make sense of things."

"And that is not the truth?" she continued to stare at him across the great, rustic den. She could feel something now, like waves of thick tangible air between them.

"Not all of it, not exactly. You see I can feel your thoughts, your emotions. Mostly they come in flashes of pictures." And then he began to move closer to her, and she could feel that thick atmosphere, the air, literally brushing against her skin before his body followed. "Sometimes color."

Her throat went dry. What was happening to her? Was this some sort of psychosis? "You're saying you can read my mind."

Then he stopped, was only a few feet from her now, quietly watching her. "It's not that simple, but yes, what is going on inside you is closer to me now."

"Now?" she questioned because it was all she could manage. It was strong the pull to him. And she realized it had always been there before but tempered somehow so that—

"Yes, I didn't want it to overwhelm things. I deliberately muffled this attraction, draw between us."

Her breathing had picked up. He was so close, and this pull to him seemed all around her now, so strong, tangible, like nothing she'd ever felt before. "James, I don't—"

"I know," he whispered, but then he was holding her arms, his hands touching her, then in the next instant pulling her up against him.

It didn't make sense, not at all. How long had she known him? How could she feel this for a few days, such a magnetizing yet calming feeling as he held her against his body? "You should stop thinking, trying to figure things out now, Mika."

She thought to answer, but he'd started kissing her, holding her, and kissing her passionately. And, of course, she was kissing him back, melting into the embrace where all thought and consideration of anything fled. And it seemed quite natural once he scooped her up in his arms and carried her out of the great room into his bedroom. Because by that moment, she felt to be someone else entirely.

"I was wrong."

It was one of those times she and her Gran would silently step into that secret room on Freret St. and simply sit in front of the painting of the Lady in the Blue Dress. She'd forgotten how quiet those moments were, how they would be content to be in stillness, needing nothing, wanting nothing, just content to sit in her presence.

And she'd never truly considered why until now.

"*Can you feel it, Mika?*" Her grandmother's voice, but she didn't seem to be speaking to her, but rather—

"Yes, inside your mind, dear one. Can you feel it?"

She was little, maybe nine or ten, but she turned to the painting on the wall. And she saw it, clearly, for the first time, a cascade of colors emanating outward from the frame of the picture, colors as she'd seen —

And then she remembered with her adult mind the people she and James had seen, the people on the downtown mall, and the energy flowing out of them.

"Yes, dear one, there is energy coming from the painting, powerful bands of energy."

She recognized it, blue-green, white, gold, and even purple pouring forth from the figure in the frame. "I think that was why I was reluctant to let her go. I always felt better when I came here, not realizing that I was absorbing some of her energy." The woman in the room with her, whom she knew as her grandmother, was speaking directly to her now.

"How can this be? It's only a painting. How can a painting emanate this degree of energy?" She was speaking to her Gran directly but from the body of a little girl. Her adult mind was in that ten-year-old body.

"I was wrong to treat your mother so badly. I took my pain out on her. It wasn't her fault. She was only a child, not responsible for my unhappiness. I drove her away, and she became like me, so unhappy."

"Gran, Gran," she whispered harshly. She didn't want to think about that, didn't want to think about her mother's pain now. "The painting, how can it emanate such energy? What does it mean?"

And then the older woman turned to her, her eyes looking strange. "You see, I wouldn't let it go, and I put her in jeopardy."

She could feel it distinctly, even as her grandmother was speaking. A chill had entered the room, and then she saw the shadow pass across the stark white wall across from the painting. But it wasn't like the shadow creature she'd seen so long ago, the one that

James claimed to be responsible for. "Mika, it's up to you now to make things right."

The first shaft of fear shot abruptly up her spine, and she saw long tendrils of dense shadow pass across the rose-colored dress that her grandmother wore. "You have to be smart, my dear," Gran's voice remained stoic as she saw the tendrils solidify into long reptilian fingers.

She turned sharply and saw it standing behind them. Tall, at least a foot higher than her grandmother, but slender, maybe half her width. The face was dark, a black and green shadow, nebulous until it settled into a garish caricature of a man with sharp, long thin features and a distorted mouth that opened on the brightest collection of white fangs.

"Run," her grandmother rasped as the thing closed its long tendrils around her Gran's throat.

With a jolt, she sat up in the bed in the house on Bleak House Road. Her heart was racing painfully. She pulled the sheets more tightly around her as she tried to calm herself. The spot next to her was empty. He'd gone. She tried to calm herself, but she could still feel the fear all over her skin. And then, out of the corner of her eye, she noted the mass of sheets and blanket on the other side of the bed flutter ever so slightly.

She edged further to the end of the mattress as she saw the sheets increasingly begin to puff up and writhe as tendrils slowly eased from beneath the mass. She tried to move but felt immobilized as more dark shadowy appendages shot from beneath the covers lashing and pinning her arms. She opened her mouth to scream, but nothing would come out as the shadows beside her solidified into that hideous man who'd attacked her Gran moments before.

"No," she managed to get out, but it was pinning her, wrapping around her naked limbs. But with an extreme force of will, she managed to wrench her hands free and grab the sides of its misshapen head. Out of blind but determined panic, she thrust her thumbs into its horrible flat, dark eyes, pushing as it wreathed beneath her grasp. Her fingers began to freeze as all she could feel was cold and mush as she drove into the back of its head.

"Mika, Mika," he yanked her abruptly into his arms, shaking her.

For the second time, she awoke in James' queen-sized bed. She looked around. No creature, just the same as it had been when they'd first fallen asleep. "Are you all right?' he demanded in a panicked voice.

"I was fighting something, something horrible," she whispered in a rasp.

"I saw you thrashing, but I couldn't reach you, couldn't wake you up."

She continued to breathe heavily, as though she couldn't get enough air in her lungs. "What's happening?"

He pulled her closer, directly against his chest. "We're running out of time."

"It's not a choice. You are selected."

He watched Mika asleep on the sofa in the den. He knew she was exhausted from the attack but adamantly refused to close her eyes in that bedroom again. She'd borrowed a shirt of his and a long robe and acquiesced to resting in the den. He sat at the foot of the couch with her feet on him and his propped up on an ottoman. But he didn't rest. He watched as the first vestiges of dawn crept in from a skylight at the apex of the ceiling.

"What do you mean we're running out of time? What was that thing?"

And how did he start explaining to her what took the balance of his life to accept?

"There are always guardians of this earth, those who travel between dimensions, ensuring balance is maintained in all realms."

He remembered he'd first heard this from his mother, then later from his uncle when he'd come of age, and for him, that was fifteen. And even hearing it in his mind, it sounded like such a fairytale. But then again, she'd brushed so close to one of the low ones last night, or could it be considered this morning? Last night they'd been so close, become lovers, and he'd forgotten what they were facing for a while.

But they hadn't. They'd felt the power between them, the growing power, and had struck hard.

She moved and murmured restlessly in her sleep. Closing his eyes, he put his hand on her leg and focused. Again, he surrounded her with a white light of protection, fending off any possible further attacks. The energy they'd created earlier helped fuel this protection, but it wouldn't last. Attrition was their strong suit, wearing down one's defenses until there was an opening.

It was not surprising that someone of his bloodline was selected, but somewhat surprising that it was him. He was an unorthodox choice, to say the least. "*It is not a position that one can aspire to or train for. The guardians are selected, and signs will appear.*"

His uncle had informed him of this after more than one sign had made things clear.

When he was five, a circle of crows appeared in his backyard at dawn. They brought the shiny goblet that now sits in his study.

When he was ten, he entered the gray forest through a dream and was gone for ten days, returning with one of his wooden staffs. Although this journey he did not remember clearly and later was convinced that it had happened during a daylight sojourn into a patch of wilderness not far from his home. Memory was like that his uncle had told him. It will sometimes compensate and fill in for what the mind was not ready to accept.

But when he was fifteen, before they began to train him in earnest, he was attacked. He was a traveler, crossing levels of reality, proficient at it. Before realizing what he was doing, he was attacked viciously by a band of low ones in the planes of a nearby realm, a concurrent dimension. In truth, he shouldn't have returned at all, but he did. They'd sniffed out his power, even when those around him were unsure about him. He returned home with the Claymore this time, the one his Great Uncle Devon Carlyle had left behind during one of his skirmishes with the invaders.

And then, at twenty-five, he'd met his wife in college. Something within drove him to turn his back on his family and obligations and seek a different life. Years later, his uncle would explain that this was part of his path. He had to understand that denying his identity would never lead to peace.

After she'd died, he almost lost his mind. He nearly descended into darkness, but his uncle stayed with him, guiding him through despair. And then, at twenty-eight, he formerly accepted his calling, was initiated, and banished into the other realms until he could find his way home.

He did at thirty, having discovered the skull of the first Magician in the land of Annwynn. At that moment, the power was released into him, changing everything.

But he was always told by his mother, by his uncle, that *"You won't walk this path alone."* He stared at the woman asleep on the sofa, wondering what she would choose, what indeed.

A Brief Respite

The first time Adele was approached was a year after Patrice was born. She had taken her out in her baby carriage to a small, picturesque park not far from her home. For Adele, the days were long and uneventful. George had returned from the war taking up a local post, and with the occasional help of her mother and a part-time housekeeper, she was solely responsible for her newborn daughter. Her days became enmeshed in the responsibility of raising a small child.

The day overhead felt gray, dismal from recent rain, and it had crept into her as a sort of depression at the thought of the life that had been snatched away from her. In fact, she was so caught up in that line of thinking that she didn't even notice when the tall, slender man in the dark suit walked up to the bench where she sat. "Mrs. St. Clair," he said with a decisive accent.

Just for a moment in excitement, her eyes flew up to his face, marking a slight resemblance. But quickly, her enthusiasm faded. It wasn't Devon. Devon was gone, taken away from her by fate or perhaps as a punishment for her infidelity but gone, nonetheless. "Yes," she answered softly.

"I've been waiting for an opportunity to talk to you privately." It was an accent, perhaps Scottish, she couldn't be sure. Devon's had been lighter, less pronounced.

She looked away, in the distance, that coldness settling in her heart that she couldn't seem to lift. "I see," she murmured.

"A relative of mine, Devon Carlyle, sent me to retrieve something he left in your safekeeping."

The stranger sat down on the bench next to her without an invitation. "And when did he ask you this, Mr.?"

"Camlin, Joseph Camlin, I was left with instructions before Devon's untimely death. You see, the painting is very precious to my family. Devon left me instructions to contact you if it were needed."

A thought dawned on her as she turned to the man next to her. "Did Devon believe something would happen to him?"

At the question, he seemed to become uncomfortable, flustered even. She recognized the emotion as she'd often seen it when she questioned George about his late-night card games with other officers. "Well, to be truthful, Mrs. St. Clair, Devon did take chances and, in some ways, put himself in dangerous situations. Of course, only when he felt it was warranted."

"I thought the car accident was just that, an accident."

"That is the official report of it."

She turned away from him, looking forward again. And at that moment, she decided she didn't want to know. She was angry with Devon Carlyle for leaving her, for making her love him, for giving her a glimpse of something that she now would never have. If he took chances and somehow got himself killed, then that was one more thing she was angry with him for. "What do you want of me?"

"The painting, Mrs. St. Clair, the Raybourne, belongs in my family's safekeeping." And then, after an awkward moment of silence, he murmured the words that Devon had told her the last time she'd seen him. "As above, so below."

Her heart dropped. Those were his last wishes. But then again, what about her wishes? After a long moment of consideration, she responded, "Mr. Camlin, I understand what you are telling me, but I assure you the Raybourne couldn't be in safer keeping than my own. It is all I have left of Devon, and I am sure he did want me to have it."

Her pronouncement seemed met with a moment of shock. He agitatedly answered, "Mrs. St. Clair, I don't think you understand. This goes far beyond a simple gift. There are elements out there that very much want to put their hands on this painting. I don't believe you understand its significance."

But something inside her had kicked in, something cold and indifferent born of heartbreak. "I'm sorry, Mr. Camlin. I can't help you."

She stood up and moved to the baby carriage, where Patrice had been quiet throughout the exchange. Still flustered, Joseph Camlin stood beside her, his eyes suddenly fixed on the baby, still silently sleeping. In a very peculiar moment, he leaned over and brushed his fingertips along the side of Patrice's face, but she still did not move. "I understand," he said quietly. And then he focused on Adele again, with an unreadable expression. "Mrs. St. Clair, I will leave my card with you," he said distractedly, fishing it out of his coat pocket, then handing it to her. "If there comes a time when you change your mind or you need anything, please contact me." And then he turned and abruptly walked away.

She watched him leave with a bit of puzzlement. And then she glanced down at the baby, who had just opened her lovely green eyes.

Around forty years later, she was contacted again by another relative, asking her to leave the painting to James Clairmont after her death. By then, Patrice had given birth to her child, Dominique. Adele poured all her attention and love into her grandchild as she had not found herself capable of doing with her mother. And as her final days approached, she did as she was asked and wrote the letter to Mika, asking her to deliver the Raybourne to James Clairmont.

Once they both finally got some sleep, they awakened in the morning, after ten, which for him was late. There weren't many words between them except for niceties and long, thoughtful silences. The truth was he wasn't sure where to begin with Mika, how to get them to the other side of this deep trench of the unknown that now yawned before them, acknowledged or not.

After a lite brunch, she opted for a shower while he dressed. He waited, trying to plan the next leg of this journey that he was hopeful they would embark upon — hopeful but not convinced. This was all new territory for him as well as her.

When she reappeared in the den where he was having his second cup of coffee, she was dressed in the clothes she'd worn the night before. It dawned on him in the moment that the events of last night felt as though they'd occurred so long ago, as they'd covered so much territory since then.

She smiled a little shyly, and it struck him how vulnerable she seemed.

"I borrowed your hairdryer. I didn't want to go outside with wet hair," she murmured.

"Outside?" he questioned.

"Yes, I think I should go back to the hotel, but I'm not sure where my coat is."

He stood up, putting down his mug. It's on the coat rack in the foyer. I put it there last night when—"

She seemed to take a breath, "When you brought me inside."

"Yes."

"Yeah, that's all a bit fuzzy. You said something about energy."

He walked closer to her, frowning, not liking the sudden awkwardness. After all, they had spent a portion of the night before in bed together. "I suppose it's natural to have some memory gaps. A lot has happened."

"Yeah, maybe, but I'd like to change."

He nodded, coming closer and reaching out to touch her arm. He just had to make contact. He thought if he didn't, he might go a little crazy. "We can go there and bring your clothes back here."

"Back here?" she said softly.

Then he put his hand on her other arm, wondering why he hadn't kissed her yet this morning. "I think so. I think you should stay here until we figure things out."

She looked at him oddly as though puzzling, "Here is where I was attacked by, well, by whatever the hell that thing was."

"We call them low ones."

"We?" she repeated.

"Yes, my family, my clan as they called us once."

"Clan? That sounds so Scottish."

"My family line, or rather our family line, goes through Scotland, France, different places, of course, here in the United States as well."

She frowned slightly, "Yeah, still trying to absorb all that. You know this is so outside my wheelhouse. I don't even know where to begin with it."

He softly touched her face with his fingertips. "Well, let's begin with us, shall we? I'd like you to come back and stay with me for a bit until—"

"Until?"

"Well, until we decide what's next. And no one can protect you better than I can."

"Do I need protecting, James?"

"Hopefully, not for much longer. I need to teach you about that blood that runs through your veins."

She took a breath, a brief respite from whatever wild roller coaster ride she'd found herself on. If it had been James just telling her things, all these extraordinary things, then she could have dismissed them as unreal, conjured perhaps from a disturbed mind. But she had felt, seen, and experienced unbelievable events. They had traveled astrally. She had spoken to her grandmother in dreams and fought off the attack of some malevolent beast, and she had felt, felt so much, ostensibly had come alive in the past few days, as though she'd been strangely sleep-walking through her life before now.

But for just a little while, it had to stop, and it did. He drove her to the Omni hotel on the downtown mall but hadn't waited downstairs for her, had come with her to her room and waited while she changed and freshened up in the bathroom, waited while she gathered her things, all of her things to take back to his house.

A few days ago, she would have never considered this. James Clairmont then had been a stranger to her but now. Now it was different. In some respects, it felt as though she'd taken a journey of a thousand miles with him. They were close, oddly close, and she wasn't completely sure why.

She disregarded the notion that it was just the intimacy. Yes, they'd slept together, but she'd slept with her ex-husband for years and never felt as close to him as she did now to James. Her cheeks burned a bit as she recalled their time, brief time together before the wheels came off of everything. It had felt so different, so profoundly more intense than anything she'd known before. To say she was falling in love with him felt somehow ineffectual. There was something more significant, some bond that didn't feel new, not new at all in fact, more succinctly just reawakened.

But this afternoon, they didn't talk about bloodlines, low ones, or profound astral journeys. He took her out to a late lunch at a small café on the downtown mall, and they just felt like a couple, a new couple enjoying their time together.

"Do you like living here?" she asked, out of nowhere really. It was just something that had occurred to her.

He glanced up from his half-eaten cheeseburger. Initially, she had ordered a salad out of reflex, but hearing his order changed hers. She wanted, needed something a little self-indulgent to get her through whatever was coming. "Huh, now that's not an easy answer. At times, I suppose, and at others, it has been isolated."

"But you felt you needed to be here?"

He nodded, "Yes, it was necessary. My time in the desert, wandering, so to speak."

"Wandering? Is that what you've been doing?"

He picked up a French fry and took a bite. At moments, she'd found him formidable, but not now, with his half-eaten cheeseburger in front of him.

"At times, do you really want to open this particular box just now?"

It bothered her because she felt sadness in those words. Was it sad? Whatever he was thinking about. "You sound as though things are ending somehow, James. I mean, that's what I feel in some respect."

He reached over the small metal diner table and covered her hand with his own. "I'm sorry. I don't mean to seem that way, Mika. I just remembered a long time ago that I had to choose which direction my life would go for basically the rest of my days. And although I have no regrets, I know that with every choice, there is an ending, a door closing."

She turned her hand and held his with her own. "You know, I just feel it's time for you to stop being cryptic and tell me what's going on."

He smiled, seeming to be rallied by her pragmatism. "That's what I like about you, Mika, your directness. But let's finish eating, then we'll take a walk."

She nodded, "And then?"

"And then, I'll tell you everything."

The Magician

His mother was very different from her brother and sister. While his Aunt Aubrey was blond, his mother Ivy had chestnut-colored hair. While his aunt and uncle had light-colored eyes, his mother had dark brown eyes but wide and deeply reflective of her emotions. While his aunt could be stern and loud at times, his mother was generally quiet, softer in tone, except during extraordinary circumstances. She was tall and willowy in contrast to the petite well-figured Aubrey, but what had always impressed him deeply about her was her strength. At times, he suspected that she was the strongest person James had ever met, which was saying a lot considering the cast of characters he'd been introduced to, even at a very young age. But Ivy Clairmont was different, perhaps in unique ways even stronger than his father, he suspected, who was supremely intelligent and formidable in his own right. Though few recognized this, perhaps even no one else but him, because she was content to let others take center stage.

He remembered clearly when he was fifteen, and he'd returned home with the Claymore that had belonged to Devon Carlyle. After a great, exhausting battle that he scarcely recalled, he'd slept for three days straight. He recalled how odd it was when he finally awoke. The house was so quiet. Usually, in the morning, he could hear his two younger siblings, Anna and Chase, clamoring about something, but nothing this morning, just pure silence.

His head was throbbing, but at that point, he was completely unaware that he'd been asleep for so long. As he dragged himself into the kitchen, he first saw his mother sitting quietly at the small round breakfast table near the bay window. She glanced up as he entered, smiling, "I thought you were going to sleep the rest of the week, James," she murmured. It was odd. His mother always called him James, no nicknames, unlike his dad, who would call him Jimmy.

He noticed with somewhat blurry eyes the spread of cards in front of her and recognized them immediately. All his life, he'd seen his mother pull out these cards, silently consulting them, then quietly putting them away. "Where is everybody?"

"Your Dad took Chase and Anna to Grandma this weekend. He thought you might need some time to rest."

"How long have I been asleep?" he remembered that things felt different at that moment. But exactly how, he couldn't quite put his finger on because everything was still awfully blurry.

Her large brown eyes settled on him firmly, this time filled with concern but something else, a quality that he later identified as acceptance. "Three days."

"Three days?" he glanced around bleary-eyed. Had it been that long? "Wow, I should eat something, but I don't feel hungry."

"You will," she said softly, smiling. "Now, come sit down. I want to show you something."

He remembered dragging himself over to the table and sitting across from her. He did ache everywhere, feeling as though he'd been beaten up somehow, but he could remember very little at that point, just flying and feeling great thrashes of pain across his skin as though he were being attacked. "You know, I know something happened, but I can't remember now."

She nodded. Her eyes filled a little with sadness. "Give it time. It will come back."

Even through his foggy mindset, he picked up on the fact that something was wrong. "What is it?" he asked directly because he knew his mom, and his mom would always tell him the truth.

"It's okay, James," she said softly, patting his hand. "I was just hoping my children would have easier lives."

He frowned, "Easier? Why, what's wrong?"

She sighed slightly, reached for one of her oversized Tarot cards, and handed it to him. "We've been waiting for the signs for a good while, my darling, the ones that point to those who will will become the Sainings."

"Sainings?" he repeated. He'd heard the word before in his presence, mostly between the adults and extended family.

"Yes," she said calmly. "They are ones who travel between dimensions, making sure balance is maintained."

He held the card in his hand. Still, just a little transfixed by what she was saying. "I know. I believe you've told me about this before."

"Yes, and the signs are now pointing to you, James. This will be you."

He remembered being dumbfounded and unable to absorb what his mother was saying. And then he looked down at the oversized Tarot card in his hand. It was called the Magician. "I don't understand."

And that wasn't a lie because he truly didn't. "It's the mantle that you will take up." And then she hesitated as though choosing her words carefully, "It's not an easy calling, James, nor is it one that can be ignored."

He stared down at the card. The man in ceremonial robes, one hand pointed up and the other down, and on the table before him was a collection of objects, including the sword. "I remember holding a sword," he murmured.

"Yes, you brought it back with you."

"Back? From where?" he said with alarm.

"From the other side."

After lunch, they'd gone for a walk in the downtown mall. Mika still felt disoriented from the night before, so much had happened, and, in response to her thoughts, James took her hand in his. She'd expected them to return to his house, but they didn't. Instead, he led her into a bookstore on the corner of the mall. Vaguely, she'd thought to question him about his motives but decided not to. The truth was she was enjoying this new relationship sort of haze that had settled upon them as though they were now functioning as a couple. Whether that was the case or not, it felt that way.

Once in the bookstore, he told her he needed to pick up something, so she amused herself perusing through the new releases until he'd gotten his purchase. And then again, he'd taken her hand in his and guided her out of the store.

She'd asked softly, "Everything all right?"

And he just looked at her with affection and smiled, indicating they sit down at a small wrought iron table at the center of the mall. It struck her oddly that this place reminded her of the French Quarter with its cafes and patios out on the sidewalks. She pulled her coat around more tightly as a cool breeze passed through. James seemed intent as he fished out his purchase from the bookstore, which turned out to be a large box of cards. She quickly recognized them as he opened the box to pull out the contents. "Are you going to read my fortune, James?" she said teasingly.

He glanced up, "Have you had that done?"

"I'm from New Orleans. Of course, I have — The Bottom of the Teacup when I was a teenager. My mom took me there, although I didn't find it particularly illuminating."

He began to flip through the cards, then stopped rather quickly. "My mom reads the Tarot. I remember it often from when I was a kid."

"She would read your cards?"

"No, not really. She would just read them herself, quietly. She said it was for guidance."

He pulled one of the cards out of the deck and placed it in front of her. She recognized the illustration style. It was the Rider Waite deck, one of the popular ones, if she remembered correctly.

"The Magician," she murmured.

"Yes," he said, tapping the card lightly. "She told me that the Tarot means much more than meets the eye. That it's very old, filled with symbols, and tells a story hidden from most."

She stared at the card, frowning a bit, focusing on the objects near the figure in the illustration. "The goblet and the wand are both in the painting of The Lady in the Blue Dress. I mean Raybourne's painting."

"Is that what you call it? The Lady in the Blue Dress?"

"Yes, that's what Gran used to call it, and so I did too."

He smiled, "Blue is a powerful color. Do you remember the energy you saw when we traveled?"

She looked at him oddly. "Traveled?" And then it came back to her on the fringes of her recollection — the two couples on the downtown mall and colors pouring out of that elderly couple, beautiful fluctuating colors. "I-I think so, James. I remember colors and feeling the power."

"Yes, you saw the energy and its vibration fracturing into color." She glanced down again at the card in front of her. The man in ceremonial robes had one hand pointed up and the other down. "As above, so below," he said quietly.

She looked up at him, a little surprised. "What did you say?"

"The figure, pointing to the sky and then the earth. That was what you were focused on."

But then he had said that, hadn't he? He could read her, flashes of pictures, emotions from her thoughts. "You are reading my mind."

"We're moving much closer, Mika. I know you can feel that."

She glanced down at the card again. There was something, something confusing.

"Not everything is there that's in the Raybourne, the crystal ball," and then she swallowed, "the burning candle and, and the skull."

He nodded, "No, it's not exactly the same. Each brings its strengths to the table. Not to be too blunt, the sword represents masculine energy, the active force. The crystal ball, the candle, represents the inner wisdom, the feminine energy, introspection."

She was breathing deeply. Why was this affecting her this way? It was just a Tarot card, but she felt a gambit of emotions running through her. "And the skull?"

He was looking at her so intently as though gauging her reactions. "Yes, the skull represents the grounding to the earth, the bloodline of the protectors."

"Bloodline?" she murmured. He'd talked about that — their relationship, her mother, Raybourne being *one of us.*

"When I was fifteen, my mother gave me this card from her deck. She said it was my mantle to carry," and then he said softly, "that ostensibly I would become The Magician."

She hesitated in confusion, "What does that mean? Would become?"

"She told me there are always guardians of this earth, those who travel between dimensions, ensuring balance is maintained in all realms."

She looked at him a little blankly, wondering if she'd even heard him correctly. "What does that even mean, James? All realms?"

He pulled another card out of the deck and placed it in front of her. With confusion, she looked down at it. The figure in the blue ceremonial robes stared back at her serenely from the illustration. She was dressed in an elaborate headdress sitting calmly between stone pillars, one light, and one dark, with a crescent moon at her feet. "The High Priestess," she whispered.

"Yes, she is the eternal counterpart of The Magician. One without the other is incomplete. The masculine energy without the feminine energy is out of balance, unable to achieve its missions, its goals. They are equals, each essential, each critical, and each ineffectual without one another."

"I-I don't understand," she murmured.

"Her wisdom spans the spectrum between the light and dark."

She couldn't stop staring at the card, "The moon."

"She remains hidden, protected, until the time."

"Time?"

"A time of reunification."

She glanced up to read his expression, but it was perfectly serious and intense, as though what he was saying was plausible. "What does this have to do with me, James?"

And then something changed in his face, a flicker of concern, compassion, many things she believed. "After my wife died, I made a decision. I chose to accept this path. I have been working for many years to keep the low ones in check, to maintain barriers that they seek to cross, but my work has been," he sighed deeply, "incomplete, easily eroded, out of balance."

She wanted to stop, stop now because somehow it felt frightening. But at the same time, she also felt compelled, as though something deep inside was pushing her onward. "You said you accepted your path. How? How did you do that?"

He stared at her for a moment, and she could feel, feel around the fringes of her consciousness, his thoughts. "I underwent a ceremony."

"What kind of ceremony?"

"I fused my energy with the energy of the original Saining. I became The Magician."

Memory

There are memories that are tucked away in a special place but always recognized as being available once you decide to reach for them. And there are other memories, considered extraneous and unimportant, that might surface in an odd moment when they are jarred back into existence by a similar recollection, only to be unceremoniously swept away again. And then, there is a different sort of memory, deliberately buried, directly entombed, deemed as threatening to one's very conception of reality, of life as it is understood. They are filled with power, sometimes a poison, that is judged too dangerous, so they are locked away in a vault, so secret, so deep that they are believed to be unreachable until they aren't.

Mika awoke in her bed, or rather the bed at her grandmother's house on Freret St., to the feeling that someone was calling her. She sat up, watching the drapes on the open window lightly fluttering with the breeze, then listening intently, but there was nothing. It must have been a dream. She relaxed back onto her pillow but didn't close her eyes because—

And she couldn't complete the thought because she didn't know. She didn't know why, except that she was expecting something.

She breathed in deeply and heard the slightest motion outside, somewhere undefinable. She concentrated on the window. She could hear the shifting of branches of a nearby tree, but that wasn't it. She focused elsewhere, canvassing her room, but perceiving nothing, silence, until finally beyond, through the wall to the wooden floors beneath the lovely chenille throw rugs that her Gran had placed in the hallway. Listening carefully, she finally understood. The wood was creaking, creaking beneath the weight of someone's feet. It was just around the bend of the stairs, down the slim hallway that led to her door. Someone was heading to her room.

She breathed in deeply, wondering if she should worry or be fearful because she knew it wasn't her Gran. Her Gran had never come to her bedroom in the middle of the night, and the clock by the side of the bed reflected 3:15 AM. And it certainly wasn't her grandfather because he seldom had much to do with her. Her mother Patrice was out of the country, traveling with her new husband, her stepfather, though he'd scarcely spent time with her. He might as well be a stranger. So, whoever was coming was someone unexpected, who perhaps shouldn't be in the house. An intruder and she should be afraid, but she wasn't.

Her eyes rested on the door, and she saw the knob turning slightly. Now might be the time to run, hide, poise for an attack, but she did none of those things. She just watched it turn with an altered state of curiosity, as though she were someone else, somewhere else, and this didn't really mean much.

And then, softly, gently, the door swung open.

Was she shocked? She didn't feel it. Was she afraid? No, not really, just oddly disconnected somehow. She didn't speak, just waited. She hadn't initiated this encounter, so—

"You have such a busy mind." Actual sound, speech, though not exactly. *"You can hear me inside."*

"What do you want?" Conveying thoughts in the same way, mentally, is not as hard as one might think.

"It's time for us to have a chat, Dominique Devalieur."

Mika continued to hold the card in her hands, The High Priestess. Her fingertips felt strange, touching it, tingling, as though there was some odd energy she was tapping into just holding it.

But that wasn't possible. So many of these were manufactured everywhere, all over the world. They couldn't all contain energy.

"It's the symbols on the cards. You're able to access them because of who you are."

She looked up at him, feeling suddenly greatly agitated. "James, look—"

"I know, I know that initially, all of this will feel upsetting to you."

"Stop," she almost snapped out at him. Then she tried to regain control, "Please, stop anticipating me, reading my thoughts, emotions, whatever it is you do. It's just getting to be a bit much."

He leaned back in the black wrought iron chair, looking at her strangely. "That's not it. That's not why you're upset."

"What?"

"You know, don't you, Mika?" he said with conviction.

It's hard to say what exactly she looked like. A concreteness of form didn't seem like the goal here. There did seem to be a figure because Mika was so young, and her eyes needed to have something to anchor to. But the exact composition of the form appeared to fluctuate into varying comforting images. It was sort of like an older woman with kind eyes, a child at times, an older sister, and then a lovely young woman in the softest velvet blue dress that felt like snow when she touched it — though she hadn't touched it, just felt keenly as though she had. The woman perched herself on the edge of Mika's bed as though they were having a relaxed but decidedly confidential conversation. And it felt good. Above all, it felt as though just her presence was putting a warm, comfy blanket around her heart that soothed so many pains that she was dealing with, even at such a young age.

"Who are you?" she'd asked in the way they communicated.

"Don't you know?" It was difficult. It was fluctuating, as though she was any comforting feminine image that Mika could contemplate at the moment — Mother, Sister, Friend — all these things and more, champion, counsel, sage, warrior.

Mika sighed deeply. "That's a lot."

"It is. I am a force, an idea, a creation, energy, whatever your mind can assimilate now." And then she reached out lightly, touching Mika's hand, and she felt it for an instant, just fleeting, where she belonged. *"One day, this will all make sense to you, my child, my sister."*

She stared at the card and then dropped it on the table in front of him. It felt calamitous, things colliding inside her at once. "I need to go," she said quickly, grabbing her purse and jarringly leaving the table. There were people around her as she walked away rapidly, but she didn't see them. All she could see was that woman, that woman from a memory she'd completely forgotten so long ago.

"Is that what you wanted to tell me?"

The woman smiled as though she understood. Even then, Mika had a defensive quality, an armor she had adopted to protect herself that would only grow over the years. *"No, I wanted to prepare you because you will find your true place one day. You will take the special energy that I am and become something more. And once you do, you will leave behind what you were before. It will be frightening because our world teaches us to exercise free will above all else and above everyone else, but that isn't what we are meant to be."*

"And when that happens, will I be happy about it?"

"It will be more than happiness, little one. You will find peace."

As she continued to rush blindly through the outdoor mall, she suddenly stopped, realizing all at once that everything around her had become perplexingly quiet. She paused, right in the center of the brick-laid aisle of the mall. There was silence, no sound from people, birds, and cars on the outside of the mall, just nothing, jarringly like a vacuum. She looked behind her, and the path she'd come from seemed to have stopped visually, like a fog she'd aimlessly wandered through. But she didn't remember a fog.

She turned around again in confusion but then froze. She wasn't alone anymore. A good three or four yards away from her, there was now a man standing there, a tall, older man dressed entirely in gray, gray shirt, gray suit. Her heart picked up its beat because, disturbingly, he reminded her of something she'd seen before in that nightmare — the thing whose eyes she's punched out with her fingers. But now, he wasn't that. He was a person, but still with the haunting resemblance.

"You're a hard woman to find, Mika Devalieur, but lucky for me, I broke in just in time."

"What is evil?"

His mother looked at him oddly, and he supposed it was an unusual question from a twelve-year-old boy who should concentrate on video games, his favorite television show, or perhaps something else on the superficial side of things. But he asked these questions because they occurred to him and often plagued his young mind.

And as long as he could remember, Ivy Clairmont had never dodged a difficult question. "Hmm, well, I suppose evil is the deliberate intent to cause harm to others."

Again, they were sitting at the round breakfast table in their kitchen. "So, there is no actual devil."

"Actual devil, horns and a pitchfork or the fallen Lucifer? I believe many have fallen away from the love of the eternal spirit, the love of God if you will, and do they become devils? Well, free will can form any of us into devils if you pursue negativity relentlessly enough."

"So, there isn't an actual evil force?"

"The force of chaos, the force of greed, the ambition to cause pain and destroy on any level, in any place, can be called evil. And it can be daunting in its determination."

He remembered that when he fought devils, demons, and low ones intent on the annihilation of anything that opposed them. Were they simply entities who had fallen and alienated themselves from grace? Hard to say. When such darkness was involved, it was often nearly impossible to contemplate its origin.

There was something wrong. As soon as he'd started explaining things to Mika, he felt a tremendous confusion and swirl of conflicting energies within her. He could feel some power beneath the surface of her skin that had been dormant before, a connection to the high priestess, to the Lady in the Blue Dress that she shouldn't have yet but still did somehow.

And then she had fled. And for a moment, he sat there stunned, trying to piece together what he was feeling. And it was that moment where he failed because he felt something else, something he'd felt a long time ago at this very mall when he'd been here with his Uncle Gideon, seeing the low ones creeping in, testing the barriers that held this world apart.

Without thought, he was on his feet, following that path she'd taken but seeing nothing as he reached where she should be. He spun around. People were everywhere, in the shops, on the street, mingling, talking, but not Mika. And worse than that, in fact, absolutely chilling, he couldn't feel her, couldn't feel her anywhere.

He cleared his mind completely and quelled his emotions. He couldn't be clouded. This was too vital. He sought her, sought her life force, sought her spiritual energy, and then finally, he could see, if only in his mind. She'd taken another path, a path in between without meaning to, and something was there with her. He didn't understand how she'd done it without the power, without the initiation. Clearly, she'd traveled between realms, between dimensions.

He dropped the deck of Tarot cards he still held in his hands and began to center inward. He would need all the energy he possessed to pierce this veil because it was clear, more than evident, that something didn't want him to make this journey.

The Sad Ones

It was cold here, colder than it had seemed moments before when she was sitting at that table with James while he showed her those tarot cards — the Magician and the High Priestess. She had to force her mind to concentrate, to remember, because there was a fog encroaching, making it so difficult to think.

She looked up at the thin man who hadn't moved, standing still before her, yards away. But her head ached just staring at him. *"You know the kind of pure energy she has, pure like frost, like snow. Have you ever tasted something perfect, Dominique?"* Her head was throbbing with pain, incredible pain at her temples now, and his voice, not precisely emanating from that figure but seeping in from everywhere. Where was she? What had happened? *"It doesn't feel like you. You aren't perfect. Just as flawed as any of them. But we knew he wanted you for something — the one who wields the sword. So, the perfect one must be close."* It pained her, whispers of his voice surrounding her, wrapping around like tight little nylon threads, pulling, cutting with tiny slashes.

"I know what you are," she whispered outward.

Soft laughter, rumbling, "Do you? Do you really? We are you, the same, your children, your creations — incessant hunger, created in man's darkest hours, a by-product of his lust for gratification." Laughter again, she squinted her eyes shut, "We are you," it repeated.

"No," she forcibly snapped out. She was becoming weak, such an effort to speak, to do anything. Then she opened her eyes again, and he/it was standing next to her — that man, an old man, with eyes that looked like flat, lifeless orbs and skin that was not just wrinkled but looked like crinkled paper laid over his face, sickly unnatural.

"No?" it repeated mockingly. "Dominique Devalieur, I'm beginning to think you are wasting time. So, I'll let you go. Just tell us now where she is."

"She? Who are you talking about?"

And then he smiled and showed his tiny little dagger-like teeth beneath his thin, colorless lips. *"The perfect one, your lady, of course, your Lady in the Blue Dress."*

"The Saining will be vulnerable until her energy merges again."

"When will that be?"

His Uncle Gideon looked grim, his eyes exuding a curious gravity that James seldom noted in his expression. This was nearly five years before, and James had already moved into the small town outside Charlottesville. "That's unknown. A lot depends on when one is found who will be able to achieve this."

Back then, they were sitting outside a small café on the downtown mall, not far from where he and Mika had had their conversation a few moments before. For some reason, Gideon Reynolds did seem to gravitate to this area whenever he visited. And James could feel why there were such tumultuous, varying energies here, fluctuating violently up and down the scale from positive to negative, such a mix.

"What about the painting? If anyone got their hands on it now-"

"They won't," he murmured. It's well-concealed and protected, and it's only a haven for the spirit, not a prison."

He frowned, staring at his uncle intently. "This is hard to understand, and I've been living this stuff for years."

His uncle looked at him sadly, "I'm sorry about that, James. I know it's been difficult, and lonely for you, but things will change."

He stared off into the distance. "I hope so. I'm not strong enough, you know, even with the power of the Saining, it's not enough. Something is missing."

"Don't you mean someone?"

His eyes narrowed in on his uncle. "You've been very opaque about this side of things. And I don't know why."

He nodded slowly, "We all have to choose our paths, James. You had a choice, and so does the other Saining. When she is ready, she will help balance things out, but we have no right to interfere with her path."

"But what if she doesn't want this, doesn't want this life?"

And then his uncle focused on him very solemnly. "Well, let us hope that is not the case."

She heard sound, not the whispers of the low one in her ears, but of the breeze around her swirling up into a low hum. "I don't know what you're talking about."

"Liezzzz," the voice scraped inside her head. "Tell usss, and we'll release you."

Involuntarily, the image of the painting rose in her mind before she could suppress it. *"No, noooo,"* it rasped around her in an increasingly painful torment. *"That receptacle is empty. The perfect one has left it. Wheeeerrrree?"* The sound screeched throughout her, and she felt its reptilian hands grasp her arms.

Yanking away, she spun apart from it violently. *"Run,"* the sweetest whisper floated into her mind. And she did, blindly turning around and running back, back down the foggy path she'd come from. It, he, whatever it was, was just behind her, directly on her heels, but she plunged forward, even though her feet felt tangled within something unseen. Living vines, like in the dream of the forest, were dragging her down, but she wouldn't let them stop her.

And then she felt a cold hand slithering its way until it covered her mouth, blocking sound. But she struggled against it, screaming, "James," she yelled out.

His hands, warm, strong hands on her arms, were suddenly pulling her securely somewhere else.

Mika felt herself hit the hard brick pathway of the downtown mall. She sprawled onto it, hands and elbows colliding with the abrasive surface. Her breathing was heavy, still panicked. And then his hands, James that she could feel so infallibly without even seeing him, went beneath her, onto her waist. "I'm going to pull you up," he said raggedly.

In moments, she was upright, then wrapped in a warm embrace. "Are you all right?" he whispered into her hair. All she could do was hug him back, then sob uncontrollably. "It's all right, Mika. You're safe now."

She was trembling. Her knees shook, but he supported her with his arm as they began to walk.

It took all the energy he could tap into to breach the barrier that the low ones had constructed. It wasn't ideal to attempt such a journey in a public space, but strangely enough, he'd found, people's perception and memory usually accommodated what their minds refused to assimilate. In other words, if they witnessed something that tampered with their conception of reality, their memory would adjust itself so that they remembered something more comfortable. If he vanished in front of them, they would simply recall him walking away. Most people would do so, though not all, he'd found.

He tapped the powerful energy within him that he'd fused his spirit with almost a decade ago. As he traveled to the nearby corner dimension that the low ones had intercepted Mika within, he could grab onto her just as she'd begun the process of traveling herself. It was clear that she was operating in sheer panic mode but also clear that she was tapping into a great well of energy neither she nor he was aware that she possessed.

All he could do in her state was grab hold and fling them back to their point of departure, both spilling onto the brick-laid street of the Charlottesville Downtown Mall. Once they'd collided on the hard surface, they'd broken apart — Mika falling to the ground a few feet away from him. It took a moment for him to catch his breath, feeling acutely as though every ounce of his energy had been wrenched from him in a battle. She was face down, and for a moment, he worried that she'd been seriously hurt.

He dragged himself up, then put his hand on her waist. With that contact, he could sense the residue of negative energy all over her. "It's all right," he murmured as he felt her stir. She was okay. He could tell through the touch, battered, yes, but all right, nonetheless.

"James," she whispered brokenly as he pulled her to her feet and placed his arm around her in support. "I-I couldn't get away."

"I know," he murmured in comfort. "We need to get out of here." He noted for the first time that they were drawing the attention of onlookers. Slowly, they began to walk back to where he'd parked his car. He felt her trembling beneath his hands that held her protectively and securely to his side.

Breathing was difficult. Perhaps it was an injury when she'd hit the ground.

"It's energy. You lost a tremendous amount when— when you left." He'd stopped himself. He'd almost said traveled, but he didn't know how much she realized, how much she understood of exactly what had happened. "You should close your eyes and rest until we get back to the house."

"I can't. I'm afraid I'll see that man—that thing. What was he?"

"One of the low ones, or a composite of many, I'm not sure." He forced himself to concentrate on the road. This unforeseen excursion had taken a tremendous amount out of him as well. "My mother used to call them the sad ones," he murmured.

"He didn't seem sad. He seemed quite gleeful, actually."

"They thought they'd won. They thought they had you."

"No, no, they didn't want me. They were trying to get at someone else," she muttered almost inaudibly, "the Lady in the Blue Dress. He said I could leave if I could tell him where she was."

"Where she was? Is that what it said?"

"I thought he meant the painting, but he said she wasn't there. What did he mean?"

"The Saining," he said quietly.

"I thought that was you. You told me you'd merged your energy with the Saining, the Magician."

"Mika."

"Yes."

"Please, just wait. Wait until we get back to the house."

She didn't answer, but he also noticed that she didn't close her eyes.

It felt like a swirl in her mind, so many memories that didn't make sense, events that she couldn't be sure had happened. Had she hallucinated it all? And James, she'd never seen him quite like this, so quiet, almost withdrawn from her.

Once they'd gotten back to the house, he took her suitcase inside, put it into the spare bedroom, and then told her abruptly that she needed to shower. "I'm too tired. I'll just change."

He looked at her with the utmost seriousness. "Mika, you've been through something quite traumatic. You've come very close to a tremendously evil entity."

"Evil? I've never heard you use that word before."

"I don't know how else to describe something that exists on such a low vibrational level of evolvement. The journey you took, the experience you had, drained you deeply of energy. At the very least, you must get the negative energy off you and see to your wounds."

She glanced down, having not even considered the fall she had after, after what exactly? "What do you mean by journey?"

"Shower first and change, then we can talk."

"James."

"Shower first. I must insist, Mika. There are towels in the cabinet." And then he'd turned around, leaving her standing alone in confusion.

Forward and Backward

James knew the first thing he should do would be shower and wash off all that negative energy from his journey to rescue Mika. But he didn't. Everything felt as though it was going off the rails. He was so overwhelmed. He had to get hold.

He had planned today to calmly explain to Mika her role in the battle he was fighting against the low ones and then bring her back to the house where hopefully, she would consent to an initiation. Then the energy of the Saining would be released and fused with hers.

But something had gone wrong, off-track, and she had physically, not through astral projection, traveled into a nearby dimension where she had encountered that composite of the low ones. But he knew she didn't have the power to do this, not yet, not without the Saining. He collapsed into his chair in his study, completely gutted. Then he remembered at the table when he'd given her the High Priestess card. Something had happened then. Something in that moment had connected with her. He'd felt it, a stirring. He didn't understand it, but he was sure something profoundly important had occurred.

He stared at the painting, the Raybourne he'd hung on the wall. When he'd first gotten it, he looked deeply and saw the energy emanating. That must be where she was, where she'd been dormant for so many years. *"Not a prison but a haven,"* his uncle had told him.

Long ago, through ceremony and the sheer will and power of creation that we all possess, Raybourne had created a haven for the spirit of the Saining to rest, rest until the next cycle of activity. James had wandered through the desert, through many realms after Cynthia had died, and then fused with the energy of the Saining when he returned. But she, this one, the Lady in the Blue Dress, was different. Her force was of opposite energies, internal, the feminine energy. They were equals, the masculine and feminine, both formidable, but one without the other was incomplete, so she was protected while she was dormant.

He stood up, staring at the painting again. *"A haven, not a prison."*

"You are not meant to see," a voice within his mind that he did not recognize. "This is not your journey, though she will meet you on the other side."

He felt something pass through him, something powerful that also felt familiar. Again, he sat in the chair, then bent his head, closing his eyes.

Mika felt confused and so tired that thinking seemed to collapse inside her. She went through the motions of showering, then dressing in just a black tee-shirt and white sweatpants, and drying her wet hair for a few moments, but not long. Such exhaustion had set in that she simply pulled it into a ponytail.

The bed in the guest room seemed to beckon to her, but she was distantly afraid of dreams of that thing attacking her again. *"You're safe."* She heard a soft voice comforting her.

She was hesitant but gave in, crawling into the bed under the soft off-white comforter and pulling the covers around her. Her mind stopped trying to puzzle things out. She was too tired. At last, she gave in and let go.

As she walked, her feet seemed to tap on the cool wooden floors of the great room, large but cluttered, filled with canvases, easels, several wooden chairs, and a few tables that her eyes scanned. They were covered with distinct tools, scrapers, brushes, palettes, scattered papers with sketches, and of course, paints — the private domain of an artist. "*Transitory, forward,*" the curious words whispered in her mind, but then a peculiar chill filled her.

There were voices disconnected from what she was seeing. "Keep your hands as I positioned them," a man muttered gruffly.

"I have to move, sir. My limbs are hurting."

"Yes, yes, one moment, I nearly have it," was the rasp. She moved toward the sound of the voices, but she couldn't see anything but the abandoned room. "It has to be exact for this to work."

"I don't understand. I've posed for other artists, and it's never been so grueling."

And then she heard a mighty crack, as though something was harshly put down on a table. "That's it. That's all I need. Change. Make sure you leave the blue dress intact, nothing pulled, nothing damaged."

"Of course, sir, yes," the sound was nearly tearful.

"Here's your pay. Let yourself out."

"Yes, sir."

And then the soft sound of footsteps clattering away. But she still couldn't see, just hear the commotion around her.

"Henry, she's only a child. You should be gentler with her." This voice was different, stronger, yet female.

"It has to be perfect for the Saining."

"It will be. Your creation will be a secret haven."

"How much time do I have?" his voice seemed hesitant, uneven.

"Not much," the woman answered quietly.

Dizziness swept over her, and her vision became foggy. She knew distantly that this must be a dream, and yet. Again, she found herself in the cold chamber, alone, but this time the painting was there. The Lady in the Blue Dress, sitting on an easel, finished. The smell of paint was strong all around her. She willed herself to move toward it and found a distinct physicality to her movements. Her bare feet were cold on the floor, and a long white shift that she wore ended just below her knees.

"She's there."

It was startling. She'd been sure she was alone, but a figure moved out of the shadows, a man. It was jarring. She'd seen enough old photographs to know that this was Henry Raybourne, although he looked bedraggled, long rumpled white shirt over dark pants, though all of it distinctly from another time. "What did you say?" she whispered, wondering for not the first time what her part was in this.

He moved closer, full beard and mustache oddly reminding her of James. "Last night, the old woman transferred the spirit of the Saining into the painting where it will rest until it is time again."

"Time?" she murmured, staring at the picture of the Lady in the Blue Dress. "How can you put something alive into a painting?"

He stood next to her now, and she could feel something flowing out of him, a skill, a power. "It is not as you think, not flat, but a new place."

"I don't know—" And then, as she spoke, she saw the colors flowing out of the painting, ribbons of dynamic color. And then a draw, a distinct tug pulling at her.

"It's all right," he murmured as she felt herself collapse into it because, in truth, she had no other choice.

"Why?" she whispered within herself and outward.

"You do not yet understand the manifesting power of creation."

She spun around the table, the burning candle, the skull, the wand, the goblet. The air around her was lightly scented with spice, cinnamon, and vanilla. But the small room stretched onward through doorways, infinitely into other hidden spaces. She was within.

"It's not so small." Behind her, she turned around and couldn't help but be stunned. The lady from the painting, the dark-haired lady in the blue velvet dress was standing there in all three dimensions with warm eyes brimming with compassion.

"How—" Mika muttered, but then she stopped. What was the question? Distantly, she remembered this was a dream, but it didn't feel like a dream. It felt as real as anything that had ever been.

"I know this seems overwhelming."

"But you're really alive?"

"Everything has life, my child. Even inanimate objects are filled with the spark of life and potential. The world you live in is not as simple as you believe. It is ever evolving, transforming."

Her mind was spinning, as was her vision, as light and energy danced off the walls of this extraordinary place. "And you are the Saining that James told me about?"

"The Saining is the fusion of flesh and spirit. I am part — "

"Part?" Mika repeated. "And this is where you have been?"

The lady smiled and then slowly placed the crystal ball on the table that Mika had scarcely realized she'd been holding. *"For a time, though, you will also learn that time is not what you understand it to be."*

She could feel that and so many things coming together, as though just being near the lady was giving her tremendous clarity of vision. "I-I can see that."

"Yes, forward and backward." Her voice led Mika through a sweep of vision where she could see her life in a great rush back to when she was born. Flashes of light and emotion, how happy her mother seemed to hold her. Her mother, Patrice, Mika actually melted into her heart at that moment, then she could feel all the conflicting emotions and the painfully lonely life she had led. And she could see the devastation and confusion as Mika's father left them. She seemed so fragile, so needing love. She'd never seen her that way before as such a vulnerable human being.

And then she could see her Gran when she was a young woman and the man she'd loved and lost, then the crash of bitterness that had settled around her heart, except for the painting. Its power had kept her from descending into collapse until there was the love for her granddaughter.

She breathed deeply, feeling waves of energy flowing into her lungs. So extraordinary, "I see so much."

"Yes, my child, and there is more."

And in a great swirl, she could see James alone in that house, flinging forward barriers against the onslaught of the low ones, year after year, alone and determined, drawing on the ancient energy that he'd taken within him, but it wasn't enough.

"Yes, you can see. He needs help."

"Help?" she repeated.

"Yes, Mika, you understand. It is you. It has always been you. He knew it when he visited you in spirit when he was young. He knew when you contacted him about the painting and when he first saw you. He's been waiting for you, as have I."

She looked at the woman, staring at her. "You're asking me to do what he did."

"To become the Saining," she said serenely.

"But he said he fused his energy. How —"

She smiled softly, and it reminded Mika strongly of something from so long ago. *"For you, it's a matter of acceptance. I've been with you a long time."*

The sight that was already hers turned back to the past. She could see herself talking to the lady in the bedroom. She had lightly touched Mika's arm that night, but now she could see that the lady had also reached out and softly placed her palm on Mika's forehead. *"I will be within you and awaken when it is your choice,"* she'd promised.

How had she forgotten? How had she remembered? It was impossible, and yet now she knew that nothing was impossible. *"It is your choice Mika,"* the lady whispered from within her.

But she'd already chosen somewhere along the way, she had already chosen, and it was done.

When James opened his eyes again, he had no idea what time it was. He stood up groggily, aimlessly wandering into the large expansive den of his house. The rustic metal clock on the wall showed just after five a.m. And he could see the morning light of dawn creeping in through the large scenic windows on either side of the room.

Quietly, he moved down the hallway past his bedroom and into the guest room, where Mika was probably still asleep. The door was closed, but he silently turned the knob and opened it. She lay there, sleeping on the twin bed, her dark hair spread around the pillows, and he couldn't help but liken her to a princess in a fairy tale.

He stood at the doorway watching her, feeling strangely even within the storm of chaos that had been the day before that somehow a calmness had settled in. He silently approached the bed, pausing at its side, and acknowledging how deeply he'd fallen in love with the woman before him. He didn't know what the future would bring or completely understood what had brought them here, but he felt genuine peace as he bent over and lightly kissed her. And at that moment, she stirred, just like Sleeping Beauty from the story, her eyes opening and mirroring his love.

Patrice Dupont sat quietly at the Café Du Monde in the heart of the French Quarter. She wasn't sure why she had come here, except that it was a touchstone, the last place she'd seen Mika, literally six months ago. She'd been trying to reach her for some time, but it was as though her daughter had dropped off the face of the earth. None of her friends, people she'd typically be in contact with, knew what happened to her. Her bills at her condo were evidently still being paid, but her neighbors said she'd been gone for some time.

She'd thought about reporting it to the police, but she had received a postcard recently, just one. "I'll be gone for a while, Mom. Know I'm Thinking About You. Love Mika." And that was it. It came from somewhere in Virginia. And it didn't sound like her. She rarely called her Mom, just had always called her Patrice as her mother, Adele, had done.

Somewhat despondently, she continued to drink her café au lait. Something strange was happening, beyond Mika, within her. She felt different inside after their last meeting after her mother passed away since Mika had left. In a curious way, she stopped running as she'd always felt she'd done her life. She was tired, and there was nothing left to run away from, not even herself. It was quiet, just quiet around her, and now somehow quiet within her.

She didn't notice his approach. She was too caught up in her thoughts until he stood beside her table, so strangely reminiscent of long ago.

"Gideon," she murmured with a great degree of astonishment. It was him. Of course, he'd aged in those years since she'd seen him, but she knew him immediately.

"Patrice, it's good to see you." She smiled with confusion. How long, how very long it had been. He was standing in front of her, dressed in a casual tan jacket and shirt and pants, nothing dressy, though he'd never really been that. "May I join you?" he asked.

She nodded, gesturing to the chair. She took off her sunglasses to see him more closely. "I'm astonished you're here. I have to confess. Sometimes I believed I made you up somehow."

He sat down across from her, smiling congenially. "I've come with a message from your daughter."

She was stunned. How did he — "Really? Mika?"

"Yes, I know it seems strange, but she's actually with my nephew James. She wanted me to tell you that she's fine and will be away for a time."

"Away?"

He nodded, "Yes, and she and James will be married while they're gone."

She looked at him, completely dumbfounded. "Married? I've never even heard of him."

He touched her hand, reminding her of a thousand memories she'd stored away in a box somewhere. "It's all right, Patrice. I can tell you that she's very happy."

She felt her throat constrict with emotion. "I'm glad. She deserves to be." She pulled her hand away and took a sip of her coffee. It was a lot, in fact, maybe too much to deal with, as was this specter of a long-forgotten love sitting in front of her now. That was the sad part. She'd realized sometime after he'd left that she had been in love with him. But, of course, by then, it was all too late.

He smiled a little sadly, almost as though he'd heard her thoughts. "Would you like to take a walk with me, Patrice? There are things I'd like to talk to you about."

She shrugged, "What kind of things, Gideon?"

He smiled as though he were genuinely happy to be with her. "I'm thinking of taking a trip to Scotland. Have you ever been?"

She put the cup down. "No, no, I haven't."

Then he gazed at her in that charming manner that she remembered, as though somehow, he was teasing her, but in a friendly way. "Well, you should see it." Then he stood up and extended his hand to her. And without hesitation, this time, she took it.

Finis

The Tethering: A Portent of Crows

6 x 9 Softcover 190 pages

ISBN 978-1613425992

Deborah Brandt's beloved Aunt Gena always told her that she was special, a bit different, and would have to live her life unlike other people. Of course, this she disregarded as the ramblings of her lovely but notably eccentric aunt. Although there were the things that Aunt Gena said that seemed true — like Deborah being sensitive to energy shifts, having potentially psychic impressions, and dreaming of a spirit guide — none of it could be real. But the most ridiculous thing that her Aunt Gena told her before she died is that there is someone special out there for her. She said that he is an extraordinary man who is not only her perfect match but someone who she would learn from so that they could help the world in difficult times. How ridiculous! It sounds like a fairy tale, and no such person exists.

Daniel Wren is unique. He has been raised and trained from a young age to hone his psychic gifts. He lives in a world unimagined by most. And he has been waiting for years to contact his counterpart, soulmate if you will. But the problem is that she is painfully unaware of the type of life that he lives and the life she would be entering into if they came together.

His dilemma becomes how best to proceed. How can he win her over and move forward before outside forces take that decision away from him?

Gravier's Bookshop

A New Orleans Paranormal Mystery (#1)

6 x 9 Softcover 190 pages

ISBN 978-1-61342-288-5

Max Gravier had no intention of becoming a recluse, but after his wife's death it seems his life is heading in that direction. He spends his time running Gravier's Bookshop on Magazine Street and occasionally on the quiet helps the police solve a crime with his psychic sensitivities. That is until he answers Caroline's call, a cry for help, out of his dreams that draws him into a fierce battle for a young woman's soul.

In this first installment of The New Orleans Paranormal Mystery series, Caroline Breslin, an amazingly gifted empath, is determined to strike out on her own and has moved out from the protection of her family home. All is going extremely well until of course she comes under siege from a devastating supernatural attack. The last thing Caroline wants is to run back to her family for help, even though she is painfully in over her head. What she really needs is a knight in shining armor or maybe just that guy that keeps haunting her dreams.

The Hotel Mandolin (#2)

A New Orleans Paranormal Mystery

6 x 9 Softcover 138 pages

ISBN 978-1-61342-290-8

Peril is wrapped up in the most enticing of disguises, in *The Hotel Mandolin*, the second installment of The New Orleans Paranormal Mystery series. It's opulent, it's classic, and it's one of the most renowned hotels nestled deep in New Orleans' famous business district, but something is amiss at The Hotel Mandolin. PI Peter Norfleet is calling out the big guns to help him investigate a recent suicide at the famous establishment — his good friend Max Gravier, a formidable psychic, and his girlfriend Caroline Breslin, a talented empath. But none of them can seem to scratch the surface of this puzzle, no one except Cassie Breslin, Caroline's clairvoyant mother, who has somehow tapped into an unexpected connection with a tragic ghost from the turn of the century. And the more she uncovers the more dangerous and malevolent the mystery becomes.

The House at Pritchard Place (#3)

A New Orleans Paranormal Mystery

6 x 9 Softcover 170 pages

ISBN 978-1-61342-292-2

Nothing is really wrong with the old Warrick House on Dante St. except that there most certainly is. Nothing is exactly wrong with its new mysterious owner except that Elise is sure that something doesn't add up. In the third installment of The New Orleans Paranormal Mystery series, with the help of the very psychic Breslin clan, Elise is about to embark on a wild rescue mission into another dimension that will land her squarely somewhere she doesn't expect, right back into her past. Right back to a childhood home whose memory still haunts her to this day -- *The House at Pritchard Place.*

Dragonflies - Journeys into the Paranormal

6 x 9 Softcover 120 pages

ISBN 978-1-88756-072-6

A powerful wizard, love-crossed ghosts, a mysterious dark warrior, and an enigmatic time traveler -- a mystical wordsmith entices you into the world of the paranormal with a collection of inspired stories. Each tale takes the journey of the dragonfly imbued with the momentum and energy of change, following a winding path that ultimately will lead you to find the truth buried beneath perception.

Treading on Borrowed Time

6 x 9 Softcover 198 pages

ISBN 978-1-61342-214-4

For Julia Moreau life seems complicated. Emerging from a failed marriage and managing a lifetime of diabetes, she lives alone in her childhood home where she communicates with the spirit of her Great Aunt Lilia. But Julia doesn't have a clue what complicated is until she is thrust into being the key chess piece in a match between two powerful men of extraordinary abilities on the wild hunt for a mystical creature hidden in the heart of New Orleans' French Quarter. Will Julia lose her soul to the karma of a devastating past life or her heart to the love of a man driven by dark forces? What is clear is that whichever way she turns she is *Treading on Borrowed Time*.

Appointment With the Unknown:

The Hotel Stories

6 x 9 Softcover 151 pages

ISBN 978-1613423608

A hotel for most represents a normal place, a predictable realm of commonality. One might even go as far to say a safe space, the reliable, where nothing particularly unusual is expected to happen. Or is it? Dimensional traveling, spirit guides, mystical storms, and soul mates separated by time are only a few of the elements dotting this supernatural landscape. Drop into a collection of romantic paranormal stories where that place of commonality is only the threshold, the jumping off point, for extraordinary adventures into the unknown.

A Quiet Moment

6 x 9 Softcover 295 pages

ISBN 978-1-61342-326-4

Jacob Wyss is caught in a rut, in fact on the verge of being engulfed by it. After an excruciating and disillusioning divorce, his life as an artist in a sleepy-college town at the foot of the Appalachian Mountains has become quiet, routine, and maddening in its predictability. One wintry day, his deep restlessness drives him out in precarious conditions to a largely empty bookstore nearly devoid of another living soul, nearly.

Aimee Marston isn't like everyone else. On the surface, she lives a sedate life working as a feature writer for a small local newspaper in addition to several other editorial jobs to help make ends meet. But just beneath, her existence is largely not her own. She is a sensitive, an empathetic psychic, guided by her calling to use her gifts to help others. Unfortunately, as a result, her secretiveness has made her defensive, protective of herself, and prevented her from having much of a life of her own.

A psychic call for help sends Aimee out on a freezing January morning where her destiny and Jacob's collide sending both their lives spiraling onto an unexpected and often disturbing track. Two lonely souls connect, not by accident, but by design. Theirs is the intersection of two spiritual paths, two lovers who must struggle to overcome the phantoms of a past life, as well as the challenges of their own inner demons to carve out an extraordinary future together.

Travels into the Breach - Accounts of a Reclusive Mystic

6 x 9 Softcover 176 pages

ISBN 978-1-61342-323-3

At first glance, his life seems quiet, serene, and even uneventful. Malachi McKellan, a 65 five-year-old widower and author of esoteric books, lives largely as a recluse in a house situated just off the banks of Bayou St. John in New Orleans. But unbeknownst to most, he is also a bit of a detective, a specific kind of detective whose specialty is psychic attacks. Alongside his lifelong companion and spirit guide Simon Tull, a nineteenth century, twenty something English gent, Malachi battles the unseen, and is an unacknowledged hero to the most vulnerable - most of the population who have no idea what is really happening beneath the surface of the world in which they live.

In this collection of adventures, Malachi McKellan and Simon Tull wage war against the most insidious elements of the paranormal. In "The Three," Malachi and Simon come to the aid of a young woman being victimized by a group of dark witches. An old apartment building is the scene of an unimaginable battle against monstrous forces in "The Lost Soul." Malachi and Simon find themselves strategizing against a psychic vampire in "Obsession," and "The Hotel" turns back time to the 1980's where Malachi confronts a demonic spirit. In "Between," a past life is revisited as Malachi attempts to rescue a beloved sister from committing her existence to vengeance, and "The Wedding" takes a personal turn when Malachi must confront painful truths while endeavoring to protect his niece from a potentially devastating union. Travel into the Breach with a pair of paranormal warriors who choose to confront overwhelming forces on a battlefield unsuspected by most.

A Ghost of a Chance

6 x 9 Softcover 174 pages

ISBN 978-1-88756-050-4

Jack Brennan, an ambitious high-powered attorney dies, only to find himself constrained to a peculiar afterlife as an earth-bound spirit trapped in an old Virginia farmhouse with a very much living, reclusive writer of campy vampire novels. Hallie Barkly recovering from a painful and disillusioning divorce has forged a career and exorcised her demons by writing under the pseudonym of Sebastian Winters. Their lives intersect, and two unconventional lovers are brought together under insurmountable circumstances. They must battle an unseen force hell-bent on possessing Hallie's life and bridge death itself to make possible what cannot be - to find a chance.

Explanations

6 x 9 Softcover 82 pages

ISBN 978-1-93493-515-6

In this, her second poetry collection, Evelyn Klebert takes us down the intricate path of a personal journey. Life with its particular struggles, pit- falls, and ultimately triumphs clearly begins to mirror a universal path, the quest for answers that we all ultimately pursue. In this reflective, esoteric collection we can all explore and seek some of life's elemental mysteries and hopefully when all is said and done emerge with some *Explanations*.

Sanctuary of Echoes

6 x 9 Softcover 338 pages

ISBN 978-1-61342-211-3

Corey Knight was more than convinced that all she could look forward to now was a quiet, reclusive life spent living out the rest of her days in her childhood home on the fringes of New Orleans' French Quarter. But the unexpected specter of her deceased father plunges her into a mad quest for a missing supernatural weapon unearthed long ago. And unfortunately, her only ally is a lost love who she betrayed.

Iain Shaw returns to New Orleans, a city he abandoned a decade before while fleeing a devastating past. Here, he is only confronted by it again in the visage of the woman he once adored — the one he is now determined to get back at any cost.
Follow them both in a wild supernatural tale of discovery and redemption as they confront and unearth the echoes of a buried and unyielding truth that once tore them irreparably apart.

Breaking Through the Pale

6 x 9 Softcover 92 pages

ISBN 978-1-88756-045-0

Breaking Through the Pale is a compelling collection of paranormal short stories by metaphysical author Evelyn Klebert.

"Contact" is the tale of a woman who life is irrevocably altered when she unexpectedly establishes communication with a spiritual guide.

In "A Grey Mourning," a disillusioned man encounters a mysterious being on the foggy streets of New Orleans.

"Dancing on the Threshold" relates the story of a woman who precariously poised between life and death takes a journey that unravels the true nature of her life.

"Isolation" is the story of a woman who inexplicably finds herself alone and disoriented in an old, quaint house on the edge of a forest. Slowly, she must piece together the past that brought her to this place and the mystical implications surrounding her predicament.

The Witches' Own

6 x 9 Softcover 124 pages

ISBN 978-1-61342-058-4

On the surface things seem quiet and serene in the picturesque coastal village of Kilmarnock, Virginia. But something unseen roams its lush forests as the past and present collide and the unthinkable begins to wreak its vengeance. Young Lucy Bonner is executed for witchcraft in the town's distant and brutal past. Her death triggers an unholy chain of events which grasp at the restless heart of novelist Peter McQuade, spurring him towards a quest to uncover the dark and terrifying truth.

The Broken Vow

Vol. I of The Clandestine Exploits of a Werewolf

6 x 9 Softcover 140 pages

ISBN 978-1-61342-133-8

In the heart of every man, there is a history. In the heart of every monster, there is a story. In this first installment of *The Clandestine Exploits of a Werewolf*, Ethan Garraint is on a vendetta that begins in the heart of the Pyrenees with the fall of Montségur and leads him to the streets of New Orleans nearly five hundred years later. But the person he chases isn't really a man anymore and Ethan has been a werewolf for almost a millennium. With the aid of a gifted seer, he is on a blood hunt that will culminate in a journey that crosses the line between heaven and earth and ends somewhere in between.

The Left Palm

And Other Halloween Tales of the Supernatural

6 x 9 Softcover 104 pages

ISBN 978-1-93493-556-9

Just when all seems well and quiet when all becomes comfortable and predictable then reality bends. Evelyn Klebert takes you to a place where ordinary life fractures into the sphere of the paranormal.

The journey begins with one woman's unstoppable quest for vengeance against a supernatural creature in "Wolves," and continues in an old historical graveyard where a horrifying discovery is uncovered in "Emma Fallon." In "The Soul Shredder" a psychiatrist's unusual patient opens his eyes to a disturbing new view of reality, while in "Wildflowers" a woman strikes up a supernatural friendship with impossible implications. And in "The Left Palm" a fortuneteller in the French Quarter receives a most unexpected and terrifying customer.

More Books by Evelyn Klebert

Considerations

6 x 9 Softcover 68 pages

ISBN 978-1-88756-062-7

Sometimes the struggle to understand the meaning and complexities of living comes down to a single moment of introspection or a fleeting yet meaningful reflection. This collection of poetry by Evelyn Klebert takes you down a winding path of self-discovery where the resolution may not always be absolute, but the journey is indeed unforgettable. It a wide and varied map of inspired poetry for your examination and consideration.

Visit Evelyn's website at:

www.evelynklebert.com

Cornerstone Book Publishers
www.cornerstonepublishers.com

www.ingramcontent.com/pod-product-compliance
Lightning Source LLC
Chambersburg PA
CBHW031303120726
47906CB00003B/869